BREAKING NEWS

JAMES H LEWIS

JAMES H LEWIS

ISBN: 978-1-7329433-3-9 (Print edition)
ISBN: 978-1-7329433-2-2 (Ebook edition)

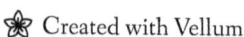 Created with Vellum

For Julie, the love of my life

CHAPTER ONE
NOVEMBER, 2008

"No, I won't!" Two people passing through the lobby of the Tribune Tower turned as I spoke. I was shouting into my cell phone, and the marble walls of the neo-gothic interior amplified my words. The overhead sculpture of the whispering man, his fingers pressed to his lips, reinforced my sense that I had committed the moral equivalent of taking my pants down in public. I retreated through the revolving door, lowering my voice as I backed out of the building. "I have been working non-stop for four months now. Stephanie and I haven't spent a single weekend together. We're on vacation. I'm not about to interrupt it."

Bartley Townes, managing editor of the *Oregon Examiner*, replied in his most measured tone. "I sympathize, Alan. You deserve time off, but something's come up that can't—" He interrupted himself. "What's that racket in the background? Where are you?"

"I'm standing on Michigan Avenue speaking with you, when I should be meeting Paul Kraus." Kraus was a former colleague who had left Portland to return to Chicago three years before. We were scheduled to have lunch together after a tour of the *Tribune* newsroom.

"Find somewhere we can talk. This is urgent."

I took a taxi back to the Hilton, calling Kraus along the way to voice my regrets. He'd accommodated my schedule, and I was pissed at having to cancel our meeting. When I returned Townes' call, I skipped the pleasantries. "What's this all about?"

"When were you returning?" From the hollowness of his voice, I assumed he was on a speaker phone.

"We're flying back Sunday evening," I said, countering his use of the past tense with the present.

A sigh at the other end. "We need you back tonight."

"Why? What's going on?"

"Alan, this is Marge Cason." She was the paper's in-house counsel. "Brill Allston has served us with a $1 million libel suit."

"Allston can't sue us," I said. "He's a public official."

"He can sue, but there's a high barrier to his winning."

"Is this about my story? It was true," I said, arguing that this settled the matter.

Bart recaptured control of the conversation. "We can't discuss this over the phone. Be here at one tomorrow. We're calling in Doons Bradberry and need to give them all the information we have on this story."

Doons Bradberry is one of the leading law firms in the Northwest. This was serious business.

"I don't get it. Allston is a public figure. Our story was accurate, documented, and sourced. He won his damned state senate seat Tuesday night, so it didn't harm him." I reeled off the standard under *New York Times v. Sullivan*—the classic case in media libel defense. "I can't imagine what he's trying to prove, nor can I see why you're in such a rush."

"They allege the story was untrue, that you fabricated it and so knew it was false, that witnesses overheard you say you were out to get him, showing malicious intent," Marge said. "If he can prove any of this, he has a case."

"That's total heifer dust."

"I'm sure it is, but we have to prove it. Understood?"

"Let's deal with it Monday."

"Tomorrow," Townes said. "If Alan Rudberg wants to continue to work for the *Examiner,* he'll be here."

Grunting an acknowledgement, I hung up, wondering what this crooked politician was trying to prove and how I could sell this unwelcome news to Stephanie.

If there is anyone out there who still doubts that America is a place where all things are possible, who still wonders if the dream of our founders is alive in our time, who still questions the power of our democracy, tonight is your answer...

Three nights before I received the phone call from Townes, Stephanie and I stood thirty yards from the stage in Grant Park as Barack Hussein Obama claimed victory in his grueling campaign for the presidency. His voice reverberated across the park as he stood before us, framed by a row of American flags. A crowd, later estimated at a quarter million, stretched back as far as we could see, but at that moment, half of Chicago seemed to have turned out on the unseasonably warm November evening.

"It's been a long time coming, but tonight, because of what we did on this date in this election at this defining moment, change has come to America." The crowd roared its approval.

"Isn't it inspiring?" Stephanie said. She drew closer. I slid my notebook into my jacket pocket and wrapped an arm around her.

I agreed with her. It was stirring, but I thought this might be the happiest night the president-elect would have in at least four years. The economy was on the verge of collapse, and the nation was mired in two intractable land wars. I doubted any of his ambitious domestic programs could rise above these immediate priorities. The urgent would trump the important.

Yet, as I looked behind me at the faces of young men and women gazing up at Obama in awe, many of their faces stained with tears, I allowed myself to feel optimistic.

It is not my nature to let emotion intrude on my judgment. I'm a reporter, the political editor of Oregon's largest newspaper, charged with providing facts and context to readers. I'm not a partisan, but rather a registered independent who has voted for Democrats, Republicans, and independent candidates for local, state, and national office.

My profession has given me access to many political figures. Some I liked but didn't think they were qualified for the office they sought; others I disliked but thought they were the best men or women for the job. Most I could take or leave. None have ever awed me. Most are ordinary people, though imbued with less uncertainty than the rest of us.

The *Oregon Examiner* had allowed me to spend a week with both campaigns. John McCain, that rare politician whom I both liked and found qualified, was open, gregarious, and quick to drop the facade behind which most political figures hide, revealing bursts of joy and his legendary anger.

Obama was cool, reserved, and analytical. It had taken some time for me to realize that this was no illusion—it was the real man. I had no personal feelings toward him; I never got that close. But I feared he was out of his element.

I respected McCain more than any politician I'd ever met—a war hero, a veteran lawmaker who knew more about the intricacies of defense and foreign policy than any of his colleagues, and a man of unwavering honesty. At the start of the campaign, I had assumed I would vote for him, but then came his choice of Sarah Palin—brash, ignorant, and unprepared—as his running mate. McCain was old and physically broken. He could die in office and be succeeded by his vice president. The Palin choice was a crucial test, and McCain had failed it.

Thus, I voted for Obama. Now, standing with tens of thousands of others on a cool, cloudless Chicago night, I satisfied myself that I'd made the better choice.

"It's a new day," Stephanie said. She was hopping up and down as she listened to the president-elect like a little girl spotting Santa Claus.

"I hope so," I said, but I wasn't buying into it. Ugly rumors had swirled during the campaign that Obama was born in Kenya, not the United States, and that he was a Muslim, as though that were a disqualification. Honest John McCain had tried to silence those of his supporters who were bandying about these false claims, but they persisted.

Birtherism, as it came to be known, was a token for racism, and when I saw some of those promoting it, either directly or by praising it with faint damns, I suspected electing a mixed-race man would not turn a new page. It might even drag racism out of the shadows, donned in a white sheet. Things could get worse, not better.

But Stephanie was euphoric, and her enthusiasm almost persuaded me. I again studied the enthralled faces of the assembled multitude behind us. *I hope we don't let you down*, I thought. And in that instant, I had the headline for tomorrow's column in the *Examiner* which I had only two hours left to write.

I was out on Michigan Avenue at six the following morning searching for a newspaper. There were none to be had. A flock of jubilant voters and souvenir hunters had descended on the city's newsstands and kiosks and stripped them of everything relevant, many discarding sports, business, and advertising sections to blow up and down the thoroughfare.

Returning to the Hilton, I opened my computer and read the electronic versions of the *New York Times*, the *Washington Post*, and my own newspaper while I waited for Stephanie to arise. The *Examiner* had one piece of unwelcome news: voters in Eastern Oregon had elected the chairman of the Franklin County Commission, Brill Allston, to the state senate. Allston was corrupt. I had spent two months investigating a kickback scheme involving contracts for everything from heavy equipment to road maintenance. Voters had read my damning story, listened to Allston's vehement denials, shrugged their shoulders, and voted him into a seat in Salem. There was no accounting for the electorate's collective amnesia. Or was it *We know he's a crook, but he's our crook?*

It was only five by her body clock when Stephanie appeared in the lobby, but she looked as though she'd spent the morning primping. "I don't know how you do that," I said. "You look terrific while I'm haggard."

"You forget I travel all over Asia for Victor Apparel. I adapt to whatever time it is wherever I happen to be."

"You should sign Obama to an endorsement contract." Victor was a leading global producer of athletic apparel, particularly shoes. They based their marketing on relationships with athletes, many of whom were black. "Obama Air," I said.

"You laugh, but I suspect his election will help sales. He loves basketball." I didn't get the relationship, but that's why I'm a scrivener and she travels the world on expense account.

"How did you land this hotel?" I asked. The Hilton lies across Michigan Avenue from Grant Park. Attending the rally had required us only to cross the street. The *Examiner* had booked us into a hotel more than a mile away; given the traffic, we might have had to either walk that distance in an unfamiliar city or watch the event on television. Victor Apparel had given us a suite and a front-row seat.

"We do enough business with this chain to get us in almost anywhere we want," she said. "Major hotels always have a room or two in reserve."

I was uncomfortable using the Victor connection. Stephanie and I keep our lives separate. The *Examiner* frequently reports on the firm, so conflicts of interest always lurk in the shadows. Consequently, Stephanie doesn't tell me much about what's going on at

Victor, and I don't tell her what stories we're researching. So far, the arrangement has worked out, and I only agreed to accept the hotel room if the newspaper paid for it.

That I was in Chicago instead of Portland was unusual. Besides the presidential election, Oregon voters had chosen between a two-term incumbent in the US Senate and his challenger, the speaker of the Oregon House of Representatives. Ordinarily, I would have been at one of the two campaign headquarters or in the newsroom coordinating our coverage, but this was not a typical year. Bartley Townes believed the likely election of the nation's first African American president was an important story. He'd packed me off to cover what we expected would be a victory celebration. The trip was also a reward for my story on Allston's kickback scheme. I'd developed this story while covering two national and two statewide campaigns. I was exhausted, and Bart thought I deserved a bonus.

Steph and I took the rest of the week off, spending Wednesday visiting the Chicago Art Institute and catching an early dinner before attending the Chicago Symphony. She was considering joining a symphony board in Portland, and I had made it my business to educate her. We began Thursday with an architectural tour, dining that evening at Moto, a funky, upscale restaurant that was as much performance art as dining experience; its closing act was *menu flambé*—the menu set aflame at the close of the meal, evaporating in a puff of smoke. We held hands, looked into each other's eyes, shared a bottle of champagne, and enjoyed one of the best evenings of our married lives. "We should do this every few months," she said.

Steph planned to spend Friday morning shopping along the Miracle Mile while I visited a colleague at the *Chicago Tribune*. We would visit the Sears Tower in the afternoon and have dinner at Spago. Saturday we would take in the Lyric Opera and dine at a French restaurant on the North Side. We would sleep in Sunday morning and catch a late afternoon flight home to Portland. It was to be a great getaway.

Then Bartley Townes called, making all these plans evaporate like the wisps of the Moto menu.

I booked two seats on a late night flight. It was full, as is always the case on Friday nights. Stephanie's upgrade miles didn't remove her from steerage, which only deepened her funk. The airline assigned us middle seats on opposite sides of the aisle, but an elderly man moved so we could be together. He might have left things as they were, for we had little to say to each other during the four-hour trip.

I had already exhausted my answers to all her questions as we packed our bags, and every answer was the same: *I don't know*. I had no idea what Allston—now *Senator* Allston—thought he could accomplish by suing us, little notion of why the *Examiner* was taking it so seriously, and even less understanding of the urgency behind Townes' demand for my return. What difference did it make whether we addressed the lawsuit on Saturday afternoon or Monday morning?

"Are you liable if he wins?" Steph asked as we reached cruising altitude over the Mississippi Rivers.

"He won't win."

"But if he does, will we have to pay?" She was playing the inquisitive journalist while I dodged her questions like a seasoned pol.

"No, the paper has liability insurance. An unfavorable judgment would affect my reputation, but not our assets."

She did not speak for some time, lost in her own thoughts. Somewhere over South Dakota, she said, "I wanted to share something with you tonight. I was so excited, but now…"

"What is it?"

"It's down to three, and I'm one of them."

I squeezed her hand. Steph's boss was retiring at the end of the year. He'd announced his plan in August and was holding on until Victor could choose his successor. Stephanie was his second-in-command, but the sports apparel company was also considering outside candidates. It didn't have many female executives, so Stephanie knew this was a long shot. "Congratulations. I'm happy for you, proud of you."

"You asked how we scored that suite at the Hilton. They wouldn't have done that for me three weeks ago, so I feel good about my prospects. Your lawsuit, however—" she said, not finishing the thought.

I didn't see what effect the paper's legal troubles could have on her chance for promotion, but at Victor, appearance is everything. "I doubt it will ever come to trial, and if it does, it will take months."

"That's not good," she said. She didn't like uncertainty, and that's what I'd given her.

"I'm sorry I ruined our weekend."

"We had a good time while it lasted." She turned back to her magazine, remaining silent as we crossed from the Plains to the Rockies and flew over Mount Hood, its snow-capped peak glistening under the three-quarter moon on our approach into Portland.

We were both exhausted when we arrived. We collected our bags, hailed a taxi, and soon arrived at our home on a quiet street below Washington Park. I unpacked, showered, threw on fresh pajamas, and tucked myself in beside her. "Good night," I said. "I love you."

She muttered something that might have been agreement or acknowledgment. It was an abrupt shift from our lovemaking the night before. Something had changed.

CHAPTER TWO
AUGUST, 2008

Those who don't know Oregon think it rains constantly. We encourage that misapprehension to keep people from moving here. In 1971, former governor Tom McCall said, "Come visit; don't stay." He lost that battle almost as soon as the words left his mouth, and as housing costs soar and traffic comes to a standstill earlier each afternoon, we relinquish more ground each day.

Oregon has two seasons: cool, cloudy, and misty followed by hot, sunny, and dry. Summer arrived late in 2008. On the first day of August, the temperature didn't reach into the seventies, and the sun remained hidden behind a curtain of gray.

Summer finally arrived on August 4. The temperature was still in the fifties when I got to my desk off the newsroom of the *Oregon Examiner*, but forecasters predicted a high of ninety-two by late afternoon. It was an ideal day to head for Mt. Hood and hike a trail to one of the many waterfalls that send torrents of water from melting snowpack cascading into streams that flow into the mighty Columbia River and on to the Pacific Ocean. One could also head west on US 26 to the Coast, turn south along US 101 to Cannon Beach, Manzanita, and on to Newport, marveling at craggy headlands and wading in shimmering tidal pools.

I would do none of that. As the political editor of Oregon's largest newspaper, I was stuck doing my job, reporting and coordinating coverage of campaigns with national significance.

Republican incumbent Gordon Smith and Speaker of the Oregon House Jeff Merkley were waging a fierce battle for US Senate. Smith, a moderate, had served two terms and should have been a shoe-in for what had long been a GOP seat, but this year, in which all-things-Bush reminded voters of the Iraq debacle and a collapsing housing market, Merkley was mounting a strong challenge. I had tracked the pair across the state since the May primaries and would continue to follow them through election day in November.

The Summer Olympics had pushed the two national conventions into late August for the Democrats and early September for the Republicans. John McCain was assured the GOP nomination, but there was still uncertainty on the Democratic side where Senators Hillary Clinton and Barack Obama had been dueling for delegates since late winter.

So when the manila envelope arrived in my in-tray, I ignored it for over an hour, and when I opened it, I didn't pay much attention at first. I finished my column for the Tuesday edition, grabbed lunch at a supermarket deli up Burnside Avenue, then returned to the office and tore open the packet.

Inside were photocopies of three paving contracts between an Eastern Oregon company and Franklin County, two more between another company and neighboring Walker County, a bid sheet on Franklin County stationery, and a finance report for a candidate for state senate, Brill Allston. I looked up Allston on our in-house database and found articles stretching back several years. He was chairman of the county commission and a spokesman for the rights of farmers, ranchers, and other interests in the eastern part of the state.

A quick glance at Oregon's map confirmed that Franklin and Walker Counties adjoined each other and were over a hundred miles south of Pendleton, the nearest population center. I inspected the contracts. One appeared to be for work on the same highway, Mascall

Road, that ran between the county seats. Others were for three more roads; one in Walker, the other two in Franklin.

The difference between the high and low bids for Mascall Road was $640,000, with a third bid midway between the two. Turning to the campaign reports, I circled the names of Allston's top donors.

Traci Jacobs was the eastern bureau chief for the *Examiner*. Though based in Pendleton, she covered stories as varied as highway fatalities, violent crimes, and local government actions across a vast swath of the state. I reached her voicemail and left a message.

Returning to our archives, I found references to three of Allston's top campaign donors. One was the president of Meredith Paving, which had won the three contracts in Franklin County. Another was the CEO of a heavy equipment company in Baker City, Eastern Oregon's largest community, a hundred miles to the east of Franklin County. The third was a Baker City contractor.

The manila envelope bore a single mailing label with my printed name and title and the newspaper's name and address; there was no return address. The postmark showed it had been mailed from Center City, Franklin's county seat. *Who are you?* I thought. *What are you trying to tell me? Are you Allston's opponent? Are you using me?*

These are the standard questions a journalist asks when a gift comes unheralded. Many people think we react to rumors, jumping into print whenever some unsourced material falls into our hands. Journalism isn't taking dictation. It requires researching public records, identifying and interviewing sources, building timelines, analyzing financial data, and only then, if all this work holds up, writing a story. Journalists are a suspicious lot, looking any gift horse in the mouth.

I dropped the clippings into a recycled file folder, uncertain it was worth a permanent investment of the newspaper's resources. It was past four o'clock when Traci returned my call. I asked her what she knew about Brill Allston.

"Not much. He chaired the county commission for at least a

decade before running for state senate. He and his brother own a cattle ranch. I've met him, but I don't get down there too often."

I read her a list of Allston's campaign contributors. She identified two more, both officials in the heavy equipment business, but hadn't heard of the others.

I described my anonymous mailing. "If these records are accurate, Allston is circumventing the competitive bidding process, awarding contracts to firms that provide campaign contributions regardless of whether they're the low bidders."

The Mascall Road project provided a telling example. "The county received three responses to its request for proposals. Grayson Paving in neighboring Walker County submitted the low bid. They had resurfaced their county's stretch of the road the previous year. Meredith Paving got the contract, however, even though it was thirty percent higher. Meredith is a big contributor to Allston's senate campaign. Taxpayers got soaked for hundreds of thousands of dollars."

"It doesn't necessarily prove anything," she said. "Anyone can make a campaign contribution. The county commission can claim Meredith's bid was more responsive, that they employed more people or had done quality work for the county over the years—any number of explanations."

We spent a few minutes discussing other anomalies in the documents, and I asked what she knew about Allston's opponent in the Senate race.

"Nate Pearson is a public school teacher who's never held office. He has some union money and support from fellow teachers and former students, but most people think he'll lose big-time."

I wondered aloud if Pearson was the source for these documents and if they were even authentic. "This seems too good to be true. I wonder if we're being set up."

"Who knows?" she said. "Politics brings out the worst in people."

"And sometimes brings out the worst people."

"Do you want me to look into this?"

I'd hired Traci out of college two years before, trained her, and given her the title of bureau chief, but she wasn't ready for the investigative work a story like this would require. "If you run across something, yes, but you have a lot on your plate, and this is speculative. I'm headed your way for Gordon Smith's campaign appearance next week. Maybe I'll stick around to look into this."

I could tell she was disappointed, but I didn't apologize. I wasn't about to have her drop everything based on an anonymous envelope with a few photocopied sheets. If there was a role for her, I'd bring her into it.

"Alan Rudberg speaking."

"I know that," my sister said.

"It's how I always answer my office phone. What's up?"

"It's about Mother." This did not constitute breaking news, but I let the thought pass. "Aren't you going to ask what's wrong?"

"I figure you called to tell me. What's wrong?"

"We have to move her," Cheryl said. "She can't live on her own in that house any longer."

"Why not?"

"It's too much for her. She needs to move into a retirement home."

I stifled a sigh. "Cheryl, I understand that's what you want to happen. Tell me why."

"When she needs to see a doctor, I have to go over there, pick her up, wait for her, and bring her home. It's too much."

"We can get in-home services to come in. You shouldn't be doing all that."

"And when I go over there, I spend hours cleaning. There's a film of grease all over the kitchen."

"You shouldn't do that either. I'll make some calls, hire a cleaning service."

"She won't allow anyone but me to come in. Mom doesn't trust these Mexican women. She says they steal from her."

"What women? I thought she won't let anyone in. And what's been stolen?" I knew where this was leading, didn't like it, and wouldn't let Cheryl get away with it without a fight.

"Nothing specifically, but things go missing."

"But you're the only one who comes in there, so no Hispanic hordes are descending on her hearth."

"She loses things. She puts them places and can't remember where she left them."

"Cheryl, this is far from a reason to take her out of her house and make her move to some unfamiliar place." A place, I refrained from pointing out, where almost all the staff would be Hispanic or—worse yet, in Mother's eyes—black. "She's only seventy years old. That's pretty young to be institutionalized."

"I'm not talking about an institution, for God's sake. I mean one of those places with individual apartments, a dining room, and a staff that's on hand twenty-four hours a day."

"Call it what you will, she's still pretty young for that."

"She's an old seventy. Have you seen her try to maintain her balance? Of course not. You're not here."

Trying to win this one was like swatting flies with a strand of spaghetti. "Have you talked with her about this?"

"You know she won't want to move. She's lived in that house ever since we moved to Austin."

"All the more reason not to uproot her if we can find a way around it. I still don't understand why she can't stay where she is."

"She will fall one of these days. That's the number one cause of death among the elderly. Falls." I doubted that but didn't have the statistics at hand to argue it. And what was the point?

"You need to come home and reason with her. She'll listen to you."

That was also untrue, and I did have the statistics to prove it. "Cheryl, I can't get away right now. There's a national election going on. I'm attending both conventions and will travel with the candidates this fall. After November—"

"Don't remind me how important you are."

"I can't come right now. Not won't. Can't."

"You always have an excuse. I've been Mother's caregiver for years. You sit there in Portland enjoying your freedom while the entire burden falls on me. It's not right."

I wondered when Cheryl had come to see Mother as a burden. Still, she was right. I was two thousand miles away. If Mother needed something, only Cheryl was there to provide it. "Decide what you need—in-home care, a lily-white cleaning service. I'll pay for it. If you don't have time to find those services, send me a list and I'll do it from here. I'm sorry, Cheryl, but I cannot come down there until after November fourth. For me, it's like the period between Thanksgiving and Christmas in retail."

Not that Cheryl had ever experienced working behind the counter at any time, let alone during the holidays.

"You need to be more supportive, after all she's done for us."

After all she's done for us.

Those words reverberated through my consciousness that evening. Stephanie was at an event, and, left on my own, I strolled through the Portland Japanese Garden near our home. The garden offers a stunning view of Mount Hood floating above the city. This evening, the salmon-colored sunset bathed the summit until Earth's shadow crept up its volcanic cone like a slow-moving wave.

After all she's done for us.

Our father left us when we were young—left for work one morning and never returned. I was six at the time, Cheryl four. One day we were a family, the next day we were not. I saw him from time to time, but Mother was always lurking in the background. At some point, he stopped coming to the house. We received no explanation, and when I asked, my mother said only, "Your father has left us."

I've not spoken to him since his last visit, although I know he lives in Jacksonville, Florida, where he's also a journalist. Did he have another woman, was he abusive, or did they simply grow apart? I didn't know then and don't now.

I cried myself to sleep for weeks, perhaps months. Mother says I wet my bed for a time, but I don't recall this. I was in first grade, and as other fathers were showing up for school events and Little League practice, I withdrew. A photo taken around this time shows a group of families at a picnic—a church outing, I think. I'm behind a picnic table, my hands stuck in the pockets of my jeans, unsmiling, observing. Who took this photo, how did Mother get it, and why did she keep it? I have no answers to these questions.

Two years after they separated and some months after their divorce, Mother moved us to Austin. The change gave me a chance to start over with new friends who knew nothing about my background. When asked, I told them my father had died in the war. This was 1967; the Vietnam War was at its peak, so this was a marketable story. It was also safe, since when asked where and how he'd died and what branch of service he was in, I said I didn't want to talk about it. Everyone accepted that.

I no longer had the luxury of feeling sorry for myself, because Mother made it clear that her load was heavier. "Your father left us with nothing. He never paid a penny to support us. I don't know how I manage."

I take nothing away from her. How she provided for us on her small salary as a bookkeeper I'll never know, but she did. She worked hard, made friends, and we were among the happy lot who never realized we were poor until we got out and earned money on our own.

But she heaped guilt and shame over us like a shroud. "He forgot about you," she said more than once when I asked what had become of him. "Why can't you forget about him?"

Cheryl dealt with this rejection by adopting our mother. She is married and has two children of her own, but Mother is her third child. She dotes on her, and vice versa.

I dealt with it by working my way through the University of Texas, landing a summer job with a small newspaper in Seguin. I worked there for a few months after graduation, then left for Portland. I knew nothing about Oregon, but a job was open on the *Examiner*, and it was as far as I could get from both parents.

It may seem a selfish move, but I devoted my life to my wife and our son, showering them with affection I never enjoyed. Eric is in his last year at Stanford and will, I predict, make a name for himself in the world of high tech that has consumed Northern California, as it may devour us all.

After all she's done for us.

Yes, Cheryl, Mother made me strong and independent and devoted to the welfare of my family. That's me—Alan Rudberg, committed husband, father, and journalist.

Senator Smith spoke in his hometown of Pendleton the following Monday. I didn't know why he was campaigning in a place he was certain to win. He'd carried every county except Multnomah—Portland—six years before and was expected to carry all of rural Oregon by a wide margin this time. I tagged along in the expectation he was testing campaign themes and to talk with locals about how they saw the national election.

Forty percent of the state's population lives within twenty miles of Portland City Hall. Those who live elsewhere in a state that measures 400 by 360 miles resent its undue influence. We talk a lot about the "two Oregons"—the urban centers represented by Greater Portland and Eugene versus everywhere else. Liberal vs. conservative, secular vs. religious, and have vs. have-not. The latter was not much of an issue in Pendleton—it does well for itself—but the remaining contrasts are ubiquitous. I got an earful that day.

"You folks are trying to throw this election," an older man dressed in jeans, a leather vest, and cowboy boots told me. "Gordon is the first US Senator from Eastern Oregon in more than half a century, and Portland wants him out."

"I'm here to find out what most concerns people in Eastern Oregon," I said, trying to mollify him and maintain my position as a neutral observer.

"We're concerned about you," he said. "Go print that."

The senator rescued me, laying an arm on my shoulder and telling my accuser, "Rudberg's a good man. He doesn't play favorites. And he's from Texas, aren't you Alan?"

"Along the way," I said. The cowboy, faux or foe, did not seem mollified, so I was relieved to head for my rental car fifteen minutes later and begin the two-hour drive south.

The Franklin County Courthouse is pre-war vintage, built of the local stone that lines both sides of the highway into town. Air conditioners hang from windows of offices on the top floor, as the central air system, added decades after the original construction, can't reach the upper tiers. I stepped into the clerk's office. A young brunette woman greeted me. She had a pretty smile, but her well-larded lower half would have her shuffling from side to side in another ten years.

"Can I he'p you?" she said in a voice so melodious she might have been a native Norwegian.

"I'd like to see the file on contract 2007-18-106," I said, referring to the road shared with Walker County.

She frowned. "And who might you be?"

County contracts are public records, open to any citizen who wants to see them, but I didn't want to get crosswise of someone who could either help or hinder me, so I withdrew my driver's license and showed it to her.

"You're not from here," she said.

"I'm a reporter for the *Oregon Examiner*."

She stuttered and looked over her shoulder for help. A slight, balding man wearing glasses with thick lenses looked up, frowned at me, and nodded toward the back of the office. The woman walked in the direction he'd indicated while the man stared at me with something I took to be resentment. I smiled and returned his gaze. He looked down.

A beefy man with thick black hair combed straight back, wearing a plaid shirt and a bolo tie, emerged from his office. "Jim Jeffreys. I'm the clerk of court. Wanda says you want to see some records."

I introduced myself and offered my hand, which he accepted, pumping my arm. I repeated my request.

"That's from last year," he said. "I'm not sure we have it on file here. It may be in storage."

I doubted that the clerk would have stored an eighteen-month-old contract that had run into the current year but said, "Could you check for me?"

He looked at me for a moment, saw I wouldn't budge, and said, "Wanda, you want to see if you can run it down?" Returning his attention to me, he said, "I think it's a pretty straightforward paving contract. Something I can help you with?"

"Maybe," I said, "if there's anything in the file that's unclear."

The older, bespectacled man pretended to be engrossed in papers spread out before him, but he listened to every word, clearly eavesdropping. I try not to judge people I haven't met, but I took an instant dislike to this fellow. Something told me he would be on the phone to Commissioner Allston as soon as I left the building.

The miss named Wanda returned with a legal-size folder stamped with a grid containing various notations. "You can sit at that table," she said, "but you can't take it away."

I opened the file and flipped through pages of reports showing proof of performance, stubs for progress payments, the contract itself, a bid sheet, the formal RFP, and copies of newspaper notices proving the clerk had advertised the RFP.

It was all there except one thing. I asked to speak to Jeffreys again while the little weasel behind the desk pretended to ignore me. "The file shows a record of only one bid."

Jeffreys turned the file around and examined it. "That's right," he said. He examined the bid sheet as though he were seeing it for the first time. "On contract 2007-18-106, we received only a single bid, from—" again he referred to the bid sheet "—Meredith Paving. Fine firm. Does a lot of work for the county."

"Why only one bid?"

"You'd have to ask other contractors, I suppose. Central City is a small town. We don't have many outfits that can do this kind of work."

"How about in Pendleton, La Grande, Baker City?"

"You'd have to ask them. Maybe this project was too small for them to come all this way."

I could almost see Weaselman's ears rising out of his head to catch every word. He could not conceal his slight smirk. I turned my attention back to Jeffreys and stared at him for a few seconds, not saying a word. Sometimes your adversary breaks the silence, but Jeffreys returned my gaze with an affable smile. *Anything I can do to help you, ask. I'll stand here and lie all day.*

I was out of my element. I didn't have enough information to challenge him and didn't want to open the manila folder and show the card I had up my sleeve. I asked for copies, waited while Wanda ran them at fifty cents per page, thanked her, and left.

I spent the night at a Best Western along the John Day River. It was a cool evening, so I left my window open to hear water gushing over the rocks. It did little to calm me. The motel had an adjoining restaurant, and half the town seemed to have turned out for dinner. I ordered a flat iron steak, chewed my way through it, and returned to my room.

"I'm glad you called," Stephanie said. "How was your day?"

"Gordon Smith sends his best."

"I think he's in trouble."

"It will be close. His flip-flop on Iraq is hurting him, though you don't sense it out here."

"I have news," she said. "Ben announced today he's retiring at the end of the year. No one saw it coming. He's stored up treasures on earth and wants to stop traveling and enjoy himself."

"And you're getting his job."

"Not so fast. He's staying through the end of the year while Victor conducts a search, but..."

"You're going for it," I finished for her.

"Do you think I should?"

"You've worked for it. You've earned it. If you want it, do it."

"It would mean big changes for us." She took me through what the position entailed. If I thought she was Victor's property now, it was nothing compared to what would happen to her if she became Vice President for Manufacturing, managing the company's world-wide network of independent producers. I didn't let the potential consequences bother me. I was proud of her. This was Stephanie's hour, and I would do anything I could to support her.

"Thank you," she said. "Not every man would react this way."

"Stephanie Brayman," I said, using the maiden name she still wore professionally, "what can I say? You're a fortunate woman, wise in your choice of mates."

"And you're a bullshit artist, but I love you."

I suppose I wore a stupid grin as I walked along the banks of the John Day before turning in. I was the fortunate one.

The following morning, I found a blank envelope that someone had slid under my door during the night. I shoved it into my backpack along with other receipts from the trip and checked out at the front desk, where the clerk gave me another statement. I had a three o'clock flight back to Portland, enough time for a quick stop in neighboring

Walker County. I tried calling ahead for an appointment but got no answer at this early hour. I would have to take my chances.

Forty-five minutes later, I reached Grayson Paving on the outskirts of Munhall. I had to wait my turn to enter the parking lot as long, flatbed trucks carrying heavy equipment and spouting columns of diesel smoke exited in an uninterrupted stream. A solid woman with flaming red hair, dressed in the jeans-and-plaid-shirt combination that seemed to be a uniform out here, stood at the counter, thumbing through what appeared to be a scheduling notebook.

"Wally's not in yet," she said after I introduced myself and asked for the company president. "I sent him into town for cigarettes. Have a seat. You want coffee? What'd you say your name is?"

I accepted the coffee and repeated my name. "What kind of name is that?" she said in a tone that suggested nothing more than curiosity.

"Swedish," I said. "My grandfather was from the north of Sweden. I never knew him."

"What do you want with Wally?"

I considered how much to tell her. I wasn't certain whether she was the office manager or something more, but she was clearly the gatekeeper. It wouldn't do to put her off. "I was up in Pendleton covering Senator Smith and stuck around to talk to some local business people." Which didn't explain why I was more than a hundred miles southeast of Pendleton at the moment, but who was counting?

"We love Gordon," she said. "He's a businessman like us. Frozen food."

"Yes, I know. He defended me yesterday from someone who doesn't like big city newspapermen. This fellow said I wasn't fit to sleep with the hogs; Senator Smith said I was."

She hesitated a second before deciding to laugh. "Oh, here he is. Honey, this is a reporter from Portland. He's come to talk to us about Gordon Smith."

"Well, actually—"

"Walter Grayson," he said, putting out a meaty paw. "C'mon in. You've met Myrt. She fix you up with coffee?"

"She did." I followed him into a small office paneled with knotty pine. "I'm not here about Senator Smith. I flew out yesterday to cover a speech he gave to the Pendleton Rotary, but I've come for a different reason."

"Such as?" A curtain descended over his display of bonhomie.

"Such as why Grayson Paving submitted the low bid on a resurfacing project in Franklin County but didn't get the contract."

His eyes narrowed.

"Do you mind if I record this?" I said, pulling my recorder out of my backpack. "I like to quote people accurately."

"Put that away. And I don't want you quoting me. Myrt shouldn't have let you in here."

"Don't get upset. I'm not accusing you of being anything but an honest businessman." He settled into his swivel chair but regarded me through narrowed eyelids.

"Franklin County issued an RFP for milling and resurfacing of a 23.7-mile stretch of two-lane roadway. Your bid was $93,000 per mile, the same as you charged Walker County for work on the same road the year before. But Franklin County gave the contract to a firm that had bid $120,000 per mile—thirty percent higher." I had committed the figures to memory and didn't have to refer to my notes.

"That cost taxpayers $640,000. Why would they do that?"

He fumbled in his pocket for a pack of cigarettes, shook one out, and lit it with trembling hands. He let out a heavy, bronchial cough, took a deep drag, and filled the air with acrid smoke. "Don't quote me." I nodded in agreement. "I have to do business here, have to get along, understand?"

"Yes, I do." Grayson looked around the small office as though seeking a way out. "I have records showing there were three responses to the RFP. Yours was the low bid. Yet when I examined the file yesterday, there was only one bid. How did they manage that?"

He laughed so hard he coughed, producing a burbling sound from deep inside. "They rejected all three bids and issued a new RFP. They changed the due date and added a few small things they could have handled through change orders to make it seem on the up-and-up."

I nodded. I got it. "But you didn't submit a bid the second time."

"Why bother? They knew what I could do the work for from the first go-round. I'd given them all the family secrets, such as they are—revealed my lowest price. I couldn't come in for less. They wanted to give the business to Meredith. I knew it, and they knew I knew it, so why take the time and trouble to rebid? I wouldn't get this contract."

"And why did they do that?"

It was the third time I'd posed a variation of the same question. He held the cigarette before him, peering at me through the cloud of smoke. "Ask them, won't you? I don't have a window into their souls."

"Meredith made significant contributions to Commissioner Allston's campaign."

"Yes, he did. So did others in his company. And?"

"And?" I echoed him and waited.

He stubbed out his cigarette, reached in his shirt pocket for another, but didn't light it. "Campaign contributions. That's what you're interested in? Anyone can contribute. There's no law against it. I do it, though not to the same tune as some others."

"There's more changing hands than campaign gifts. Is that what you're saying?"

"I'm not saying anything. You're the reporter. I lay asphalt."

He stood and offered me his hand. The interview was over. "Mr. Allston will be our next state senator," he said. "It may seem a step down from commission chairman, but the state has a lot more money to spend than Franklin or Walker Counties. I may not like the way other folks go about their business, but I know only one way to run mine. I hope you appreciate that."

I did. Walter Grayson wasn't a coward; he was a realist. His clients were not only local governments but also other businesses whose owners supported local politicians. If he crossed Allston, he could say goodbye to his company. He was an honest man, but he was no hero.

So what did I have? I pondered this during the three-hour drive back to Pendleton. Brill Allston was shaking down local contractors for campaign contributions and for something more—something suggested, but undefined. Bribes of some sort. Money going not only into his campaign, but also into his pocket.

But that was an assumption based on the unspoken hints of a man who refused to serve as a source. I had no evidence to go on, nothing more than a raised eyebrow. I would need to bring a shovel to Central City and dig, but I didn't even have a treasure map.

I returned to Portland that afternoon, convinced the trip had been a waste of time. I hadn't determined whether Wally and Myrt were an item, so I couldn't even peddle their story to *People* magazine.

There were three statewide races on the ballot that year, and I spent the next week trailing candidates for secretary of state, then followed Jeff Merkley on a swing through Southern Oregon as he tried to unseat Senator Smith.

The last weekend in August, I attended the Democratic National Convention in Denver, covering the Oregon delegation. Although the party billed it as an open convention, Barack Obama finally seemed to have the nomination secured, and his opponent, Hillary Clinton, acknowledged as much when, during the balloting, she rose to ask the convention to cast a unanimous vote for the Illinois senator, thus making him the first African-American candidate for president from a major political party.

The morning after Obama's acceptance speech, Senator John McCain, who was assured of the Republican Party's nomination at its convention the following week, named Alaska Governor Sarah

Palin as his running mate. I had never heard of Palin, so I called Mindy Sergeant, a former colleague who now covered state government for the largest newspaper in Anchorage.

"You and everyone else," she said when I explained I was trying to get background on Palin. "So are we."

"Meaning?"

"She's immensely popular, but she often undermines her own party, and she's changed some of her positions with little explanation. Take the Gravina Island Bridge project—the 'Bridge to Nowhere'. She defended it at first, then canceled it in the name of responsible use of Federal funds, kept the Federal funds, but continues to build a road to the bridge. It's never clear where she stands on things."

"What are her positions on national and international issues?"

"Who knows? She's never shown much interest in anything outside Alaska, save for a trip she made to visit our reservists in Kuwait."

"This should be interesting," I said.

"Trust me, it will be wild, but you know what I think McCain has done?"

I didn't, but neither did I have to prompt her for the punchline. "He's elected Barack Obama."

I thought about that as I prepared to leave for the GOP convention in the Twin Cities. Brill Allston and Franklin County were the last thing on my mind on August 30 as Hurricane Gustav roared toward the Louisiana Coast. Working at my desk at home, I entered a month's worth of credit card bills and cash receipts in the *Examiner*'s expense form. I had two receipts from my stay at the Best Western in Central City; one handed to me at the desk and the other in the envelope slipped under my door. I entered the charges from the first, placed the receipt upside down in the neat pile to my left, slit open the sealed envelope, and was about to toss it in the wastepaper basket when I saw it wasn't a receipt at all. It was a typed message with neither a salutation nor a signature.

Jeffreys lied to you today. He's covering for Allston. They rebid the project to make sure Meredith got the work. Meredith bribed Allston. It happens all the time. Ask them where's the beef.

Where's the beef? It was the tagline in an old commercial for a fast-food chain. What was it doing here?

I thought back to the day I had spent in Central City. I'd visited the courthouse late in the afternoon, checked into the Best Western, gone for a walk, had dinner, and turned in. During the night, someone had slipped this note beneath my door. I hadn't been hard to find. The Best Western is the only hotel in town. Someone could have spotted me walking along the bank of the John Day or sitting in plain view at dinner.

No, the question was not *how* I'd been found, but rather *who* had found me. Someone who knew about my visit to the Courthouse, knew what I'd been after, knew what I'd expected to find in the contract file, and wanted me to know that the answers were not in that folder.

There was only one person with all that knowledge.

CHAPTER THREE
SEPTEMBER, 2008

Hurricane Gustav roared ashore on September 1, tearing up the Louisiana bayou, then drowning the southeastern part of the United States. Republicans opened their national convention in St. Paul on the same day—Labor Day—the latest a political party had ever met to nominate its standard bearer. To respect those undergoing Gustav, the GOP called off politics for the day, mourning the dead and dying as a way to avoid dealing with the climate change that was causing it. Democrats would have done more. They would have railed against the Republicans for not addressing climate change, but since their convention had ended, they failed at the vital task of scoring political points.

The Republicans nominated John McCain for president and Sarah Palin for vice president and listened, enraptured, as she gave a taste of what was to come. "Here's a little news flash for all those reporters and commentators," she said. "I'm not going to Washington to seek their good opinion." She did not get to Washington—not, at least, in the way she had hoped—but she made good on her promise to avoid getting favorable marks from pundits.

McCain, however, did, saying to Senator Obama and his supporters, "We'll go at it over the next two months... But you have my respect and my admiration. Despite our differences, much more unites us than divides us. We are fellow Americans, and that's an association that means more to me than any other."

After eight years of twisted rhetoric from George W. Bush, McCain was refreshing, but the star of the show was Palin, who would wander away from the convention and the campaign, forging an independent path toward political oblivion.

I returned from St. Paul and almost immediately flew out to join the Obama campaign.

Here's a secret. When reporters tell you they are "traveling with" the candidate, that's what they're doing. Except for the privileged few from broadcast networks, cable news, and national newspapers, we reporters board a second plane that leaves after the candidate takes off and passes him in the air to land before he does so that we can record his triumphal entrance to the next campaign stop. We stand in a pen at his rally and either head to the airport ahead of him or check into a hotel to pray for a few hours' sleep before the process repeats itself the following day.

Most of us may interact with the candidate only once or twice during the week and are allowed to interview him only if our state or region are in play. Which Oregon was not. The entire West Coast was going blue that year, and everyone knew it. California was big enough that its reporters got face time with the candidates, but I did not.

So why bother? Because it's expected. The candidates want publicity, the public expects news media to cover them, and journalists want to be present at the moment of creation. We're there to raise issues with the candidate that matter to our city, state, or region—things not addressed on the national stage. If we're lucky, we may learn something new, gain insight, and pass it along to our readers.

But during the entire week I spent "traveling with" Senator Obama and later with Senator McCain, not once did I extract a paragraph, sentence, or word on the burning issue of the day back home—which *was* a burning issue. Beginning with a lightning storm in early

August, the Gnarl Ridge fire had consumed hundreds of acres on the northeast slope of Mt. Hood, threatening the historic Cloud Cap Inn. Firefighters thought they had it licked by the end of the month, but in mid-September, smoldering mulch ignited again. Over 3,000 acres were burning, filling northern Oregon and southern Washington with an acrid, choking haze.

No candidate mentioned it. The issue remained hidden behind a smokescreen.

His name was Ralph Weaver, not "Weaselman," and his name was not the only thing about which I'd been mistaken. The Franklin County website listed three employees in the clerk's office. One of them had placed the envelope beneath my door at the Best Western that August night. Jim Jeffreys lacked the motivation, and Wanda Cramer lacked the insight. That left Weaver, who'd listened to every word of my conversations with the other two, and who I had wrongly suspected of serving as a pipeline to Brill Allston.

You always wonder how to approach someone who has information they want to share but is too frightened to come forward. Depending on the circumstance, I either confront them in the open, surprising them by turning up unannounced, or contact them in advance and assure them of anonymity. Here, the right course was the latter, with the implicit threat of the former.

I dialed him at home—rural people list their numbers in the directory—introduced myself and encountered dead silence. "I need your help," I said.

"We open at 8:30," Weaver said. "I'm about to leave now."

"Not public help. The other kind, the kind you've twice offered me."

He paused before replying, and with that hesitation confirmed what I suspected. "You're mistaking me for someone else."

"No, I'm not. You're bothered by what you've seen, or you

wouldn't have written me last month. I want to help you do what's right, but I can't do a story based on a few sheets of paper that may or may not be authentic."

"I can't get involved." It was more a plea than a statement.

"I'll treat you as a confidential source. You know what that means? I can't write a story on the word of one person, so I'll find other sources. That will give you cover."

He went silent again.

"I don't want to come to the clerk's office if I can help it."

"No, absolutely not!"

"We need to meet somewhere no one will recognize us. I have to be in John Day this Saturday. Meet me for coffee at Maizie's Diner, and we'll figure out where to go from there."

"Saturday," he repeated.

"You can tell me where the beef is," I said. He allowed himself a chuckle and hung up.

Apart from some babysitting jobs in high school, my sister has never held down a job. Cheryl married Tom Davis when she was nineteen, a union born of necessity. He worked for a small company that made add-on devices for the IBM PC. The firm soon began building PC clones, outgrew the garage, and began its expansion into the billion-dollar industry it is today. As Tom has grown with the company, he and Cheryl have graduated from a small apartment on Austin's east side to a sprawling home near Lake Travis overseen by a jolly woman named Manuela and her gardener husband Esteban.

Their two children are grown. With few responsibilities and abundant time on her hands, Cheryl lacks an appreciation for what life is like for us drones. Thus it was no surprise that she began her phone call without asking if this was a good time.

"Where have you been?" she said. "I've been trying to reach you."

Rather than responding that I had twice returned her call only to listen to a recorded voice telling me that the party had not set up their voicemail, I said, "Hanging out with Obama."

"No, seriously."

"I was traveling with his entourage for six days. I get to sit in the back of the bus with McCain in another couple weeks."

"He's our next president. Have you met Sarah Palin?"

"No, and I don't think I'll have the opportunity."

"She's so inspiring. Mother and I love her."

"I'm sure she appreciates it," I said. "You called."

"When are you coming home? We need to do something about Mother."

This is home. No, don't say that. "Cheryl, we've covered this. I can't get away until after the election. There's too much going on."

"You have time to run around the country with that Muslim but have no time for your family."

"Cheryl, where do you get this crap? Barack Obama is a Christian. And what if he were a Muslim? What difference would it make?" Though I knew the answer to that one.

"His father was a Muslim, and that makes him one forever. I read it. It's the same with Jews and Catholics. You can't unconvert."

"I'm aware that you can't change most people," I said. "Covering all these candidates is my job. That's why I can't come to Austin right now."

"I need your help. Mother has become too much for one person to manage. I can't do this alone."

I thought for a moment. I needed to do something to help her, but traveling to Central Texas at the moment was out of the question. "I'll discuss this with Stephanie. Maybe we can move her up here. We can find her an apartment nearby—"

"She could never live with all that rain."

"It's eighty-two degrees right now, and the sun is shining." I didn't mention that smoke from the fires had turned the sun orange.

"And Mom doesn't like your wife. She thinks she's conceited."

"Steph always speaks well of her. And you, too." Both were lies.

"Besides, Austin is her home. She needs to stay here. She needs me."

And I don't need this. I thanked her for calling, said I had a visitor, and rang off before she could remind me of all that Mother had done for us.

Oregon has two towns and a river named for John Day. Not bad for a member of the Lewis and Clark Expedition who lost his clothes to an Indian party during the trek west and his mind during the return. One town is along the Columbia River near Astoria, the other in Central Oregon on US 26. It was the latter that pulled us eastward from Portland one Friday evening in mid-September. Stephanie and I spent the night with friends at Black Butte. I left at dawn for the three-hour drive east, which took me past the stunning beauty of the John Day Fossil Beds. (I forgot to mention them. Neither Meriwether Lewis nor William Clark have as much named after them.)

I arrived at Maizie's early, took a table near the window, and ordered a cup of coffee. Ten minutes after the hour, I decided Weaver had stood me up and went to the restroom to rid myself of the coffee. When I returned, he was standing in the middle of the restaurant looking conspicuous. "I thought you hadn't made it," he said.

"Wouldn't have missed it." I sat him at the table and thanked him for coming.

"You're sure you won't mention my name."

"You are a confidential source." Once more I explained what that meant, outlining my protection under Oregon's Shield Law. "To the extent I can, I use sources to send me to public records and rely on them for my stories. I also interview others. I will neither mention you nor refer to your involvement unless I receive your permission."

"It's a small community, and I need the job. If I lost it..." He turned both palms upside down as though water were running through them.

"Where's the beef?" I said.

"There was none. That was the point."

I looked at him without expression, waiting for the punchline. "It's all here," he said. He laid a fat manila folder sealed with a string tie before me. "A contractor wants a job in Franklin County, a vendor wants to sell a piece of heavy equipment, someone wants a contract of some sort, they respond to an RFP. Then they have to talk to the commissioners."

"Commissioners?" I said, emphasizing the plural.

"Yeah, they're all in on it. You don't think one of them could do that alone and the others not want a piece of it?"

"Good point. So what happens?"

Weaver wrinkled his nose as though he smelled something noxious, but all he was doing, I recognized when it happened a second and third time, was repositioning his glasses. "I'm not in their meetings, so I don't know how it goes down. Maybe Allston doesn't even have to ask. Maybe the vendor raises the question. 'How much will it cost me?' Something like that."

"A bribe."

"Sure. A contribution gets made to the next political campaign—that's all legal, I think—but some money or some *thing* changes hands, and the contract goes through."

A campaign contribution is illegal if it's part of a shakedown, but I didn't interrupt his narrative. I was more interested in what went into the pockets of Allston and his fellow commissioners.

"Money or *things*, you said."

"Yeah, one construction firm built a swimming pool on Allston's ranch two years ago. Other times it's cash under the table."

"But where's the beef?" I said.

"Like I told you, there wasn't any. Allston's ranch is up toward Pendleton. His brother runs it while Allston runs the government." He snorted and wrinkled his nose again.

"Meredith Paving bid on three separate projects in Franklin County. The owner knew he had to pay a bribe, but he wanted to deduct it. He couldn't just fork over money. You can't list a bribe on your tax return. To make it sound legit, he needed to buy something. So Allston sold him eleven dressed steers, about fifty-five hundred pounds of prime beef he declared as Christmas gifts for clients."

"And where was the beef?" I repeated.

"There was none." Weaver smiled and chuckled to himself. "Allston and his brother didn't deliver as much as a pound of hamburger. It was a sham."

I laughed along with him. How I'd misjudged this guy. "Mr. Weaver—"

"Ralph. My friends call me Ralph because that's my name."

"How do you know they delivered nothing?"

"Look for yourself. It says right there. 'Delivery date TBD'—to be determined. I have a friend at the ranch who says he would have remembered a delivery of that size." I took down the name he gave me, but Weaver pledged me to silence.

"Ralph, how did you come by this?"

He didn't answer. I suspected he'd broken into Allston's office at night and photocopied the records. "Why did you do it?"

He pulled his glasses down to the end of his nose and peered over the frames. "I'm for good government."

I was certain the man had an ulterior motive, but he would not reveal it. I hoped to hell it wasn't a ticking time bomb.

"You have everything I can give you. Don't contact me again."

"I won't unless it's absolutely necessary," I promised.

He rose. "I have to leave now. My mother needs me."

"I understand. Mine does, too."

I wanted nothing more than to lay all the receipts and communications out on the table and paw through them, but I couldn't do that in a public place, and there was nowhere between John Day and Black Butte to stop. I drove westward again with a mounting sense of anticipation. Someone had handed me not the story of a lifetime—Franklin County was too small to serve as a high point in my career—but a story of real significance.

It would take work to develop it. I had to make certain the documents were real, and that wouldn't be easy. I needed to speak with those who'd paid the bribes, and they would be reluctant. Some would fear prosecution, others would resist crossing a powerful political force in their little universe, and one or more would likely alert Allston that I was investigating.

But the threads were there. I needed to tie them together.

I paused at the Sheep Rock unit of the John Day Fossil Beds to watch a towering cumulonimbus cloud gather over the Mascall Formation, a wall of volcanic rock laid down 15 million years ago that cascades down a long mesa in diagonal striations, whose patterns change with the angle of the sun. In this part of the state, the view is matched only by the Painted Hills fifty miles to the west. The clouds boiled and frothed from the distant horizon into billows far above the formation. I resumed my journey before getting drenched, but outside Dayville—also named for John Day, come to think of it— sheets of water descended from the sky, obscuring the road. I crept on for another fifteen minutes until it cleared, revealing nothing ahead but blue sky. Central Oregon is a constantly changing art installation.

Nearing Prineville, I got cell service back and found a voicemail from Stephanie asking me to meet her in Bend. It's a beautiful, grown-up cow town on the eastern edge of the Cascade Range, crowded with California migrants driving up housing costs while creating a demand for what have become Central Oregon's best restaurants.

I met Steph and our friends at a seafood restaurant in the Old Mill District along the Deschutes River. Bob and Nancy Sawyer wanted to know what I thought of Obama. I made some noncommittal remarks about his presence before crowds, grasp of the issues, and ability to reach across races and generations. "We have two good candidates this time," I said. "The nation can't go wrong."

"We need no more foreign adventures," Bob said.

"I think they're both more cautious than President Bush," I said.

"We need a change," said this lifelong Republican. Anecdotes are not data, but that was when I knew Barack Obama would win the presidency and that a blue tide could carry Gordon Smith out to sea.

"They're good people," Steph said as we drove through the gathering dusk across the Santiam Pass.

"The best." We rode in silence for another ten minutes, savoring the last traces of sunset. "I have to head back to Eastern Oregon next week. I'm working on a big story out there."

"Big story? In Eastern Oregon?"

"It's an oxymoron, isn't it?" She didn't pursue it, and I offered nothing more. That's how we work. Compartmentalized lives.

"I've been invited to join the board of the Portland Symphony," she said.

"I didn't know you cared for classical music."

"Victor wants its executives involved in the community, and the PSO is among the most prestigious organizations. Mark Fisher has asked me to join the board. The neurologist?"

She stated it as a question, and I shook my head. I didn't know him. "He and his wife, Wendy, are super committed."

"Wouldn't you do better finding a cause that interests you? Something with a connection to young people?"

"You don't want me to do it?"

"I'm not saying that. Do what you need to. Does this mean we get to attend symphony?"

She sighed. "I suppose so."

"What would you think of moving Mother here?" I said, broaching something I feared might be a third rail. "Cheryl says she can't live on her own anymore. She's frantic."

"Your mother doesn't like me. She thinks I'm a snob."

"Who told you a thing like that?"

"She did." We drove silently for another two minutes. "Whatever you want to do is fine with me."

In late September, the US economy was on the verge of collapse. The subprime mortgage crisis served as a catalyst to reduce liquidity. Businesses could not borrow, something they routinely do to cover such things as the gap between orders and payment. Treasury Secretary Henry Paulson had proposed a rescue plan to Congress, but many balked at "bailing out Wall Street" in an election year.

On September 24, McCain said he was suspending his campaign to work on a Congressional solution; he called on Obama to do the same and to cancel their debate scheduled for two nights hence. The Democrat declined, the debate went on as scheduled, and the economy slouched toward Armageddon.

I was working with our business editors to coordinate coverage of what this meant to Oregon. Its economy depends on international trade—shoes, engine parts for airplanes, soybeans, computer chips, timber, and a host of other products. The real estate market had dropped through a trapdoor in parts of the state where people had leveraged their incomes to buy second homes—Bend, Southern Oregon, the Oregon Coast.

By day I worked on political coverage and by night on the file I'd received from Weaver. There was no question that Allston and his cronies were running an elaborate kickback scheme, but measured against what was going on in Washington, it seemed inconsequential. Nevertheless, I persisted. The morning after McCain and Obama met in Oxford, Mississippi, I took a flight back to Pendleton, rented a car, and drove south.

At one, I sat in the office of Hal Meredith, owner of Meredith Paving. In contrast to Walter Grayson, Meredith seemed more like a golf pro than the manager of a firm using heavy equipment to gouge out the earth, lay gravel over the roadbed, cover it with asphalt, and mash it into a smooth, black ribbon. On his wall, a diploma from the University of Oregon hung next to an award from a local service club. Business books lined his shelves, interspersed with faded photos of toddlers and youngsters and more recent photos of young adults and grandchildren. Meredith had closely cropped, sandy hair and wore a pale green Victor sport shirt, chinos, and loafers without socks.

"What can I do for you?" he asked.

I made small talk about the economy and its potential effect on Eastern Oregon, then got down to business. "You bid on a contract to repave Mascall Road last year. You weren't the high bidder, but you got the work, anyway."

"We were the sole bidder, as I recall. We have lots of contracts out here."

"You were the high bidder on the first round, but the county rejected those bids and issued a new RFP. You didn't alter your original quote—$120,000 per mile for a total of over $2.8 million—but this time you were the only bidder."

"I remember. There was a timing issue, and I think realignment of a stretch along the river at the Walker County line. These things happen."

"The county could have accepted the low bid and issued a change order. Why didn't they?"

"Ask them." He shrugged and picked up a ballpoint pen, snapping the top in and out.

"Why did they pick you and not the original low bid from—" I shuffled papers as though searching for the name "—Grayson Paving over in Munhall?"

"Again, you'll have to ask them, but Grayson isn't local and can't do a job this size."

"He did a seventeen-mile stretch of the same road over in Walker County the year before. Their commission is happy with it. It looks the same to me."

"You're an expert on roadwork, are you?"

"I drive on them all the time. You made a big contribution to Commissioner Allston's campaign for state senate."

"There's no law against that."

"And all your officers made similar donations."

"Did they? That's their business." He placed both hands flat on his desk and peered at me for a moment. "What's this about?"

"And you bought eleven dressed steers from his ranch," I said. "Fifty-five hundred pounds of beef, plus kill and processing costs, for a total of $24,750. That's a lot of meat. Some freezer."

He leaned back in his chair, folded his arms across his chest, and seemed to look at a point behind me. "I don't care to discuss this anymore."

I handed him a copy of the invoice which I'd encased in plastic to resemble evidence. "Wasn't this an outright bribe to secure the paving contract?"

"Goodbye, Mr. Rudberg."

"With you or without you, I'm writing the story."

He redirected his gaze to the window, to his parking lot, to whatever lay beyond it. "Franklin County is a close community. We work together to get things done. There are formal rules and informal rules. I'm a businessman. I follow the rules I'm given and provide quality work."

I asked him a few more questions, but he provided no answers. The interview concluded, I snapped off my recorder. "Were you taping this conversation?"

"Only for note-taking."

"You didn't tell me you were doing that," he said. "I think that's illegal."

He was right. I held it up and erased the conversation. "I apologize," I said. "It's gone."

"It better be."

The drive to Baker City took more than an hour, but the day was clear, and the view of Rock Creek Butte in the Blue Mountains was stunning. Silvio Bernardo, president of Bernardo Construction, welcomed me into his office. He was a tall, gangly man in his late fifties, with a mane of curly silver hair that stopped just above his neckline and a neatly trimmed mustache. Like almost everyone I'd encountered in Eastern Oregon, he wore jeans, but his were pressed, he polished his brogues to a luster, and he wore a yellow tie over a blue, button-down shirt. I would have put money on my suspicion he was ex-military.

I'd called ahead and explained my business. Bernardo was willing to see me and proved to be more forthcoming than Meredith had been. Since he was further removed from Franklin County, he could afford to be. He had been the low bidder on an RFP to rebuild and reinforce sections of a concrete dam at Franklin County's reservoir, but he told me he'd had difficulty getting the county to execute the contract. He admitted that his company had excavated the hole for a swimming pool at the ranch Allston owned with his brother.

"Did he ask you to build it?"

"It wasn't direct, if that's what you mean. He visited here, said he wanted to talk about our bid, that he'd heard we do good work but wanted to make certain we were the right company for the county."

"Is this typical of the way government contracts are negotiated here?"

Bernardo snorted and smoothed his mustache. "You kidding me? It was most unusual. I wouldn't expect the county commission chair to negotiate a contract. He's got staff for that. And they wouldn't come to me. I'd go to them. Ordinarily," he added.

"So how did the swimming pool come up?"

Bernardo smiled. "He hemmed and hawed, talked about our work and other projects we had done, but I could tell that wasn't what he was after. Then he said, 'You folks do swimming pools, don't you?' I said we did. He said something to the effect that his brother had always wanted one for their ranch, how much did they cost, did we work up in that area, knowing full well that we did. I got the drift."

"And?"

"I told him we could build him one. Gave him dimensions. He

wanted something bigger, so I agreed. He asked how much. I said I thought we could come to some arrangement. He thanked me and left."

I let the implications percolate for a moment. "He never directly asked you to build the pool?"

"No, but I knew what he wanted."

"He never said, 'You build me a pool and I'll give you the contract?'"

"No, he's not stupid."

"But you built the pool, and the contract went through." He nodded. "Which came first?"

"As soon as we showed up at his ranch, the county sent over the paperwork."

I thought about it. If I could find similar examples, it might be enough.

In Pendleton the next morning, a heavy equipment salesman told me of leaving an envelope with two thousand dollars in hundred-dollar bills sitting on Allston's desk when he left the office, contract in hand. "Did you expense it?" I asked.

"No, but the company reimbursed me."

"How did Allston request the money?"

"He said it was customary to contribute."

"Contribute to what? His campaign?"

"'To contribute' is all he said; I knew what he meant."

I had lunch before heading to the airport for my three o'clock flight. As I was finishing my meal, a younger man with a thick thatch of blond hair approached my table. I saw others swivel their heads to follow his progress. "Nate Pearson," he said, extending his hand. "Do you mind if I join you?"

"I'm leaving," I said to Allston's opponent in the general election campaign.

"I'll walk with you." He trailed me to the front of the restaurant like a hunting dog. "I know what you're working on. When will you publish?"

"How do you know what I'm working on?" He grinned, but didn't answer. Perhaps a contractor had notified him. Maybe everyone in the district knew. He wasn't saying.

"Do you have anything to tell me?" I asked.

"It's all true, everything you've been told. It's been going on for years, but no one can prove it. We're depending on you."

Several older men dawdled in the lobby as they entered, trying to snag a fragment of the conversation. It made me uncomfortable. Not that I was speaking with a candidate—that's my job. But this encounter coming at this moment could make it appear that my investigation was a creature of his campaign.

"Mr. Pearson," I said, not being obvious about it but speaking loud enough for the men to hear, "I'm not working for you or for anyone else. I'm a reporter. There may or may not be a story here. If there is, you'll know when I publish it. It was good to meet you."

"Sure," he said, and flashed me a conspiratorial grin.

CHAPTER FOUR
OCTOBER, 2008

I traveled with McCain during the first week of October. The Senate had passed a financial bailout plan with both presidential candidates on the winning side of the 74-25 vote. McCain knew the economy would tank without an infusion, but he also knew right-wing voters opposed it. So while voting for the rescue, he tried to blame Obama for the failure of a compromise plan in the House, then backtracked, saying no one was to blame. All this flailing cost him the two-point advantage he'd carried out of the convention; he now trailed by five points.

Sarah Palin didn't help matters when she went on a $150,000 shopping spree in Manhattan, tearing through Barneys, Bloomingdale's, Neiman Marcus, and even down-market Macy's at the expense of the Republican National Committee while flubbing an interview with Katie Couric of CBS when she couldn't name one newspaper she read. She blamed Couric for asking the question.

The Straight Talk Express had been shunted to a siding, but McCain spent half an hour with some of us local yokels. I liked the guy and didn't care for what he was doing to himself, but it wasn't my job to save him. As though I had the influence.

Returning from the trip exhausted, I recalled Hubert Humphrey being asked during his doomed 1968 presidential run if the result of a campaign wasn't to crown the survivor. Humphrey hadn't bitten, extolling the joys of campaigning in what one newspaper called "a love song to America." I didn't think McCain shared the joy. I certainly didn't.

I spent another couple of days following Merkley and Smith, Oregon's two senatorial combatants, before returning to Portland to pull together the last threads of the Franklin County story.

While I didn't have everything I needed, I had all I was likely to get. Traci Jacobs had driven to Central City to secure a copy of the original RFP for the Mascall Road project. Jim Jeffreys, the clerk of court, gave her the runaround, maintaining that since the county had canceled that RFP without issuing a contract, it wasn't a public record. It took Marge Cason's intervention with the county attorney to shake it loose. Traci's visit consumed a day of her time, but the exercise convinced us that the county had plenty to hide. I also had documents, admissions by some that they'd paid Allston to secure contracts, and more circumstantial evidence.

What I needed was Allston's reaction. I called to get an interview with him, but a spokesperson said he was unavailable. I tried a second time and got a more direct response—"the commissioner has nothing to say to the *Examiner*." Traci secured his schedule, and the two of us decided to corral him after a campaign event the following day in Pendleton. I flew in that evening, and we reviewed the evidence we'd assembled. "He'll deny everything and attack us," she said.

"Yes, but we need to give him the opportunity to do it—or say whatever's on his mind."

She agreed, then said, "Alan, I need you to look into something for me. The legal department won't return the renewal on my office lease. Is something going on I should know about?"

"Not that I'm aware of." I allowed myself a sigh. Half the staff spent its day trying to meet deadlines while the other half felt no sense of urgency about anything. Office leases weren't part of my job description, but I was her boss and promised to look into it rather than making her fend for herself from two hundred miles away.

At the retirement home where Allston was speaking, we stuck out like Mormon missionaries in a nudist colony. Allston was over six feet tall, a rangy man with a head of black hair combed straight back from a widow's peak, partially concealing long ears, and a lopsided smile resulting either from a mild stroke or a permanent smirk; I leaned toward the latter. He was in full sales mode when we entered, making sweeping gestures with his right hand, a wide grin plastered on his face, promising how, as a state senator, he would protect health care and push to end the state tax on retirement income. Half the group listened while the other half struggled to stay awake, waiting for him to end so they could resume their bridge games. "I see we have the press with us," he said.

Every waking head swiveled our way.

"You're going to read a lot of stuff about me over the next couple of weeks. This is a hot shot from Portland." He enunciated the city as though it were an incantation to evil spirits. "They've chosen their candidate, this liberal schoolteacher. The leftwing press is always trying to undermine those who share our values. Just keep your eye on them and, when November fourth comes, do what's right."

He smirked in our direction as the group muttered among themselves. I feared they might cane us to death or gum us into submission. When he finished, we tore after him as he bolted out the door. "Mr. Allston, I have a few questions."

"Talk to my staff," he answered.

"A Baker City businessman says he had to build a swimming pool on your property to secure a contract to expand the county maintenance facility. What's your response?"

"It a lie. I know nothing about a swimming pool."

"A contractor says he had to pay a $5,000 bribe to sell the county a backhoe."

"County legal staff does contracts, not me."

I threw a third question at him, and he turned on his heel and advanced on me. "This is all garbage, and you know it," he said. He pushed his face within three inches of mine. "You print one word of that, and I'll have your ass in court before you can recite the Goddamned First Amendment. You got that?"

"May I quote you?"

"You'd better." With that, he entered the passenger seat of a Lincoln and slammed the door. His aide gunned the engine, throwing a spray of dust at us.

"'No comment' would have been sufficient," Traci said.

Working from my home office, I heard the television playing in the living room as I wrote my story.

"I can't trust Obama," a woman said. "I have read about him, and he's not, he's not—he's an Arab."

John McCain took the microphone from her. "No ma'am," he said. "He's a decent family man, a citizen that I just happen to have disagreements with on fundamental issues, and that's what this campaign is all about."

I could sense the air go out of the room. It surprised even his campaign staff, I later learned. It was pure McCain, a decent guy, a man of principle. I was appalled that anyone harbored such thoughts and would express them in public, proud that a candidate had the decency to respond, angered that he had to. Many later criticized McCain for not saying, "And what difference would it make if he were?" But he'd said the first thing that came into his head to diffuse the situation. Many politicians wouldn't have tried. I turned back to my story.

In Franklin County, officials often require that companies seeking to do business with the county "pay to play," providing kickbacks to members of the county commission and its chairman, Brill

Allston, a local rancher and chairman of the county commission who is running for election to the Oregon Senate.

That's according to confidential sources within the government and contractors who say they are forced to make campaign contributions and under-the-table payments to secure business with the county, even when they submit low bids on requests for proposals.

A three-month investigation by the *Oregon Examiner* has disclosed a pattern of corruption, including kickbacks and bribery. One business owner told the *Examiner*, "You can't do business with Franklin County unless you're willing to grease the wheel."

A contractor who submitted the low bid on a major repaving project found himself cut out of the process after the opening of bids. The county rebid the project, awarding the contract to the previous high bidder after he'd paid $24,750 to Commissioner Allston.

The payment was ostensibly for a shipment of beef from the commissioner's ranch, but records show that the beef was never delivered, a fact confirmed by a former employee.

I worked through the night, checking notes, listening to quotes from my interviews, and arranging documents the graphics editor would include with my article. I reported our parking lot confrontation with Allston but did not embellish the story by including how he had goaded us before the retirees.

In the morning, Stephanie found me slumped over my keyboard. When I awakened the computer, I found a string of gibberish trailing off from the last line I'd written, a track my forehead had made as it came to rest on the keyboard. I was glad for my habit of saving my work at the end of each paragraph.

Steph and I had a pot of coffee while she ate a bowl of fruit and I painted peanut butter onto a slice of toast. "Big night," she said.

"The biggest."

"You're in town Friday, aren't you? I've invited Mark and Wendy for dinner."

"Mark and Wendy...?"

"Fisher," she said. "From the symphony board."

"Can we include Bartley and Evelyn?" I'd been trying to get my managing editor to the house since early summer but hadn't found a time when Steph and I were together.

"No, not this time. I need to build this relationship. Mark knows many Victor executives. He's trying to raise my profile."

"I think your profile is fine," I said. She stacked the dishes without responding. The conversation was over.

I washed up after myself, returned to the office, wrote three more paragraphs, hit save, and sent the text off to Bartley. By the weekend, the paper would distribute the story throughout the state. Then Allston could make good on his threat to see me in court where, I hoped, I would appear as a reporter and he as a defendant.

"We need to move Mother," Cheryl's voice was shrill, reflecting panic. "You need to fly down tonight."

"Cheryl," I said, "I cannot get away until after the election."

"By then it may be too late."

"Please calm down. Tell me what's happened?"

"Mother fell last night." I had been only half listening to her familiar jeremiad but was suddenly attentive. "She lost her balance in the dining room."

"How is she? Is she in the hospital?"

"No, she's at home. She's all right, but it scared her."

"I'm sure it did. Let's get home healthcare in. And a walker. We need to get her a walker."

"She has one. She won't use it."

I didn't conceal my exasperation. "If she won't use it at home, she won't use it at a retirement home."

"At least she'll be able to alert a staff member. So when are you coming?"

"In November," I said. "I cannot leave until after the election."

"You are heartless. Leave everything to Cheryl. Cheryl will take care of it." And she hung up.

I gave it ten seconds' thought, then called my mother. "How are you?" I said.

"I'm fine. How are you?" I heard laughter in the background. People were yelling. Others were cheering. "Mom, would you turn that down, please? I can't hear you."

"I'm watching my program."

"I can tell." She turned the sound down. She treated her TV like a jackhammer, opening it up to a full-throated roar that made the floor tremble. "I hear you've had a fall."

"Who told you that?"

"Cheryl says you fell in the dining room last night."

She paused before answering. "She said that? I stumbled, but I steadied myself on the dining room table. I did not fall."

"Mom, level with me. Did you fall over?"

"I just told you. My foot caught on the leg of a dining room chair. I stumbled but caught myself. I did not fall. Ask your sister. She saw the whole thing."

I doubted I would ever learn the truth. "I'm relieved," I said. "It sounded serious."

"She wants to move me into a retirement home, has she told you that?"

"Cheryl is concerned for your welfare. She's trying to help."

"She wants to move me out of my home and into one of those places where the food is bad and they tell you when you have to wake up and what time to go to sleep. And all the people there are old."

"They're not all like that, Mom. The kind of place we're considering is like having your own apartment, only with staff there to help you if something goes wrong."

"So you're a part of this, too." Mother doesn't miss much.

"We've discussed it, but we're not forcing you into anything."

"Well, I'm fine. I've been on my own ever since your father left, and I can manage now. I raised the two of you on my own. He left us all alone, no financial support, no presents for you kids, not even a card at Christmas. I did it all."

"Yes, you did, Mom. I'll come see you next month. We'll have a nice visit and talk about all this. No one will make you do anything."

"I knew I could count on you, Sonny. Don't you let that sister of yours push me around."

I sat at the end of a conference table, flanked by my managing editor and our in-house counsel. Bartley Townes had already read my story. Marge Cason was going over it, and not for the first time.

"You haven't named many of your sources," she said.

"They fear retaliation—not only from Franklin County, but from other counties whose officials might not want to do business with informants. Their other customers are area business people, many of whom support Allston..." I left the thought unfinished. Marge is no fool; I didn't have to explain the workings of good old boy networks.

"Still," she said. She continued to read, underlining passages with a red pen. "Is law enforcement looking into any of this?"

"Not to my knowledge. I've asked a source in the AG's office if she knows of any corruption investigation underway in Eastern Oregon. She doesn't."

"Would she tell you?"

"If they were looking into something, she wouldn't comment at all. This was a flat no."

"It would be helpful," she said. "'The *Examiner* has learned that Oregon's Attorney General is investigating allegations of corruption...'"

"We don't have that," Townes said.

"I understand. I'd just feel more comfortable if someone were out on the same limb."

Townes and I looked at the table, reluctant to make eye contact lest she felt caged. Marge is a great attorney, and she's *our* attorney. She works for the *Examiner* and sees her job as trying to further publication while keeping us out of trouble. Outside counsel are risk averse. Their cautionary approach often restrains publication.

"The person who supplied you these documents, I assume he works for the county."

I didn't answer, and she didn't expect me to. Weaver was a confidential source. I hadn't shared his identity even with Townes. That's how it works.

"How did he get them?"

"I'm not certain."

"You didn't ask?"

"I did. He chose not to tell me."

"So he may have stolen them." Again, I didn't answer, though I knew some of these documents hadn't come from a public file.

"Well, we're okay, though I'm not sure your source is. The Supreme Court ruled in *Bartnicki v. Vopper* that the First Amendment protects us from publishing pilfered documents as long as we neither participated in nor encouraged it. Still, if Allston takes us to court, he'll make a big issue of that before the jury."

"That will be a reach," Townes said. "He's a public official, we've pursued the case fairly, we've asked him for his response—"

"Repeatedly," I broke in.

"Several times," Townes said, as though he were editing the formal response. "We have no history with him, so he can't claim we've acted maliciously."

"And you taped all your interviews," Marge said.

"All but two. Grayson refused to be taped. I failed to advise Meredith I was recording our conversation. He caught me. I erased it in front of him."

She moaned. "Let's hope he doesn't make an issue of it; technically, you broke the law."

I acknowledged as much. She asked a few more questions, then said, "Let's go with it."

Bart and I smiled and thanked her but avoided doing high fives in her presence.

"Marge, there's one other thing," I said. "Traci Jacobs tells me her lease is up in two months, and she can't shake the paperwork loose from your office. Can you help her?"

She stared at her file folder before answering. "It's under review," she said.

"What does that mean?"

"Alan," Townes said, "we're looking at the costs associated with every bureau in the state. Nothing's been decided yet. If it were, we'd tell you. But we won't make a three-year space commitment until we've completed our review."

"You might close the bureau?"

"I'm not saying that. We might ask people to work out of their own homes, co-office, that sort of thing. We're operating at a loss and being cautious about long-term commitments, that's all."

"What should I tell Traci?"

"Say nothing at the moment."

"Bart, I'm her editor. She's asked me to look into this. I can't ignore her."

"Tell her you've asked about it. I'll let you know when we've decided, all right?"

It was not all right, but I was in no position to argue.

Mark Fisher and his wife arrived promptly at seven Friday night bearing gifts, two bottles of Napa Valley cabernet and one of chardonnay. I greeted all five of them.

It was a crisp night. I had the gas fireplace log ablaze. Stephanie had decorated the house with orange and brown globes meant to remind us of fall. Halloween was a week away, the election only three days after that. I wasn't certain what frightened me more, ghosts and goblins or political campaign ads, which filled so much television airtime that they crowded out content.

I uncorked the white wine, filled glasses, and passed them around. Mark raised his and said, "To Stephanie." We all drank to that.

"How long have you been on the symphony board?" I asked.

"About two years. Wendy and I made a five-figure gift, and they asked me to join."

"Do you attend every concert?"

"Lord, no. We try to hit it five or six times a year. They have a great pops schedule."

"I used to play," I said.

"Oh? What instrument?"

"French horn. I always wanted to be Barry Tuckwell when I was younger."

He looked at me for a moment and said, "That's nice. We're so lucky to have found Stephanie. She's a rising star at Victor. I hope she'll be able to bring them along as a sponsor."

Stephanie made a small noise I took to mean fat chance. "Paul's mostly into sports activities," she said, referring to their founder.

"But maybe the youth concerts. Well, never mind. I'm sure we'll find something to excite him." *An evening of college football fight songs*. I kept the thought to myself.

"On behalf of the board, I thank you, Alan. You and Stephanie have been most generous."

"I'm glad to hear it." I was not, but sensing that Stephanie had made a sizable commitment, there was little I could do about it.

"Stephanie is such an asset to the PSO," he said, laying it on with a trowel.

I glanced at Wendy Fisher, who had been quiet during this exchange. "Are you in medicine, too?"

"She was," her husband said. "She was my nurse for several years, and now she's my wife." Which meant, I supposed, that she wasn't expected to do anything more, not even speak for herself.

"I'll throw the steaks on," I said. Wendy offered to help, and I let her tag along for the company.

It turned out she wanted to discuss music. "Have you ever heard of John Graas?" she asked.

"Sure, the jazz horn player, although didn't he play with the Cleveland Orchestra for a time?"

"He's from Dubuque. My dad went to high school with him. He once brought two friends over from Chicago and played a concert in our front parlor." Her laugh sounded like the tinkling of a triangle.

We talked about Graas and music and Portland while I awakened the mashed potatoes from their slumber in the crock pot, shook asparagus over a few tablespoons of water in a sauté pan, topping them with butter and shaved Parmesan when the last of the liquid evaporated, and pulled the steaks from the oven.

I asked how long they'd been involved with the symphony. "Mark gets these enthusiasms. He wants to *be* things. At the moment, he wants to be chairman of the symphony board. The moment they elect him, he'll lose interest. He'll want to be something else."

I laughed. "I know a lot of politicians like that. Why Stephanie?"

"Mark is counting coup. No one from Victor has ever served on the symphony board. He ran into her at a chamber meeting, started talking with her, discovered she was trying to get involved with a nonprofit, and asked her."

"Does he like classical music?"

She laughed. "He's into heavy metal."

"Well, a tuba..."

"What are you two laughing about?" Steph said as we entered the dining room carrying platters.

"Nothing," she said. *There. Take that. Make them guess.*

The three of us chewed while Mark rhapsodized about the wine —his wine. "The grapes came from a 400-acre plot 1,200 feet off the valley floor. They were harvested at 25.4 brix." He stuck his nose in the glass, held the glass up to the light, and only then took a sip. "Hmm. Cherries and chocolate with notes of tobacco and cassis." Our small cellar was stocked with Oregon pinot noir and chardonnay, but I was certain it didn't measure up to Dr. Fisher's standards.

"Steph says you have a big story coming out," he said.

I paused and looked toward Stephanie, who studied the gold rim of her plate. "We're publishing a little something on Sunday. I'm not at liberty to discuss it."

"Political?"

"That's what I do, politics and government."

"Will it embarrass someone?"

"Could be. This cabernet is excellent," I said. It was the right bait to draw him off the scent.

"Please don't do that again," I said to Stephanie after they'd left.

"He wanted to know what you do. Besides, everyone will know on Sunday. Even I will."

"Oregon is a small town with long roads. You never know who knows whom. If the subject of this story were to find out we were discussing him over dinner, he could make something of it—suggest I was bragging about bagging him. I don't discuss stories until they're published."

And then, I thought, I let them speak for themselves. "What did you think of the wine?" I asked.

"It was all right. Why?"

"The moment I sampled the aroma, I thought the grapes came from a 400-acre plot 1,200 feet off the valley floor, harvested at 25.4 brix. I detected flavors of cherry and chocolate with notes of tobacco and cassis."

"Are you mocking Mark?"

"No, I'm just reading the label." I handed her the bottle. "Steph, you're a brilliant person, independent, a star. Let no one highjack you. Find out what you're interested in and pursue it. Don't let others lead you around. Make them follow you."

"You don't want me to join the board."

"If that's what you want, do it. But you've never expressed much interest in classical music. Kids are your thing. We have two museums for youngsters here, adoption agencies, recreational centers, special advocates for children whose parents are in family court, a mentorship program for African American boys, and nonprofits that help kids in war-torn regions. There must be something there that speaks to you and your company."

"You think I should do that?"

"I think you should pay no attention to Mark and even less to me. Be yourself. As Oscar Wilde put it, everyone else is taken."

My story ran in the Sunday paper. It was not the banner headline— this was Eastern Oregon, after all, of concern to few, the paper felt— but the story did begin above the fold. I read the comments online. I'd stirred barely a ripple. None of the local newscasts referred to it that evening, and they're adept at rewriting our stories. Perhaps they didn't have the time or resources to fly someone out to Central City to stand in front of the courthouse in the freezing weather and tell what we had uncovered. Perhaps they had no stock footage of Allston. No video, no story.

I arrived in the newsroom Monday morning expecting the story to sink ignominiously from public view. By noon, however, a surprising source burst out of the darkness to keep it alive.

"Allston Denies Kickback Charges," read a dispatch Traci Jacobs sent us. Allston had held a news conference at the courthouse in which he'd blasted the *Examiner* and me. Traci had listened in by phone, then Allston had called her.

"He is pissed," she said. "He claims you put words into the mouths of your sources and bragged about how you were out to get him."

"Rubbish," I said. "I wonder what he thinks he's accomplishing by stirring up a story that's fizzled." But that was rhetorical. We both knew what he was up to. Brill Allston was running against the liberal Portland media, circling wagons in Eastern Oregon to repel big city infidels. First Portland was out to defeat the region's US Senator, the argument would go, and now they were poking their heads into a local senate race with lies, lies, lies.

Still, I laughed it off.

CHAPTER FIVE
NOVEMBER, 2008

I n any other year, I would have been at the headquarters of one of
the Senate candidates or in the newsroom coordinating coverage
on election night, but 2008 was no ordinary year. We sensed that
Barack Obama would become the first non-white president in US
history, and Bartley Townes, who warmed himself on the embers of
belief that the *Examiner* had influence beyond its circulation area,
thought we should be at the Chicago rally where history would be
made.

It was a lark, so I'd brought Stephanie with me to lap up the
wonders of America's most approachable major city. I seldom had the
chance to give her a perk in my line of work, and I would not waste
this one.

I'd spent the day at Obama's headquarters on Michigan Avenue,
watching young campaign staffers work the phones with state
campaign directors, who worked the phones with city and county
headquarters, who reached into the bowels of each precinct to get
supporters to the polls. It was something short of a well-oiled
machine—I could hear the occasional grating of metal against metal—
but it was the closest thing I'd ever seen. I wrote up this "B-copy"
before watching the first returns and heading across the street to

Grant Park but discarded most of it as I pounded out an early morning column in the living room of our suite while Steph slept.

Now, summoned home by a nervous boss and in-house counsel, it seemed like weeks since the euphoric faces had strained to get a look at the man who would become the nation's 44th president. Stephanie was annoyed that her visit had been cut short, I was angered that Brill Allston was using the courts for payback, and we both felt that the air had been taken out of our personal balloons.

I arrived in the newsroom at 12:30, checked my email, opened real letters, and set a few things aside to answer later. At 12:55, I entered the paneled boardroom on the fifth floor, a room where journalists seldom tread. Bart and Marge were already in place, both dressed informally as Oregonians are on weekends except for the most somber occasions. Marge introduced two attorneys from Doons Bradberry, Asa Miner, whose parents, I gathered, had a vicious sense of humor, and Benjamin McAllister

"We all know why we're here," Marge began.

"No," I said, "I don't. We investigated a county official and state senate candidate over allegations of corruption. We interviewed business people in Eastern Oregon who described how this official solicited campaign contributions, cash payments, and gifts in return for county contracts. We sought his reaction before publishing; other than threatening us, he refused to respond. The *Examiner* ran the article. He won his race, so the story did him no harm. I understand we have to defend ourselves against this suit, but why we've retained outside counsel—? No, I do not know why we're all here."

The four of them looked at each other. Asa Miner broke the silence. "Mr. Allston—Senator Allston now, I suppose—makes several charges. He says the documents we published were fabrications, his opponent supplied them to you through an intermediary, you knew this or had reason to know it, your accounts of interviews were fabrications, and you did not seek permission before recording witnesses."

I copped to my failure to alert Meredith before recording him, explaining that it was an honest mistake, but the rest of the allegations, I said, were lies.

"Allston also says you met with his opponent to coordinate your investigation and that several witnesses heard you promise to ruin him. He alleges that you failed to exercise due diligence, ignored pertinent facts, and had malicious intent. He ticks so many boxes in *Harte-Hanks Communications v. Connaughton,*" Miner said, referring to a case in which a news organization had lost a libel case, "that this newspaper runs a real risk. And that is why we're all here. Questions?"

"It's all untrue."

"That's not a question."

"Asa," Marge Cason said, "Alan returned from Chicago late last night. He hasn't heard all this."

"And that will not help," the attorney continued. "Why was the political editor of the *Oregon Examiner* attending the victory celebration of the Democrat candidate for President rather than remaining here in the state doing his job?"

"*Democratic,*" I said. "*Democrat* is a noun. *Democratic* is a modifier. I was covering the *Democratic* candidate."

"Again, why?"

"Because I sent him there," Bart Townes answered.

"That may be worse. It suggests the newspaper had a pro-Democrat bias. Understand, I wasn't asking that question for myself. It's what a good defense attorney will ask." If Miner wanted to silence me, he'd done so.

"Let's get down to business," said McAllister. "Start from the beginning and tell us how you began this investigation."

I explained how I'd received an envelope containing what appeared to be bid sheets, contracts, and campaign reports, that I'd paid little attention to it at first, but that, when other business took me to Eastern Oregon, I'd investigated the enclosed documents. I described the stone wall I'd encountered at the county clerk's office, my interview with Walter Grayson, the Walker County paving contractor, with Hal Meredith, and the subsequent tip I'd received on how a competitive bidding process had produced only a sole bidder.

They listened and took notes, asking enough questions to urge me on. I was describing my return to Franklin County when Asa Miner interrupted. "Why did it take you all that time to pursue this?"

"I was busy with other stories. I spent a week with each presidential candidate, then followed Smith and Merkley around the state. I wasn't working solely on Allston."

"So you weren't devoting that much attention to this important story."

"I wasn't sure there was anything to it at that point. It was one thing among many."

"Asa is playing prosecutor again," McAllister said. "These are the questions you're likely to get when you're on the witness stand. He—or she—will question every decision you made, every lead you followed, anything you ignored. You need to be asking yourself at every moment, what are the implications of what I'm about to say?"

"I returned in September to gather more information. I'd identified who had given me the original material, so I contacted... that individual."

"Who?"

"I can't tell you that. It's a confidential source."

"You'll have to tell us."

"I won't."

Bart broke in to explain about confidentiality agreements, but Miner waved him away. "I appreciate your ethical stance, but this is the guy—I'm assuming it was a guy..."

I tried to stare him down.

"He was the source for the documents you published. He's an issue in this lawsuit, so we need to learn all we can about him."

"I don't reveal my sources."

"We don't," Bart said.

The two attorneys looked at him, then at each other. "All right, let's try this," McAllister said. "How did you identify him?"

"By a process of elimination. I knew who had access to certain information and knew who had been present during my conversations with others. When my informant revealed something that could only have been learned during one of those conversations, I was able to identify that person."

They asked a few more questions, trying to get me to reveal more, but I played rope-a-dope. "Did you ask how he'd come across the documents that suggested Allston had received bribes?"

"Yes," I said. "But the individual wouldn't say. I assume my source got into Allston's files somehow and copied them."

"No!" Miner said. "When you're asked that question, stop at 'he wouldn't say.' Don't suggest you knew he stole them."

I sighed and stretched my arms. "I need a break. It's been a long week."

I hit the men's room and then found a fifth-floor window that gave me a view of Council Crest. "I understand your frustration," Marjorie Cason said. I was so engrossed in wishing I were up in the Japanese Garden, I hadn't noticed her approach.

"I'm trying to decide whose side they're on."

"Ours," she said, "believe me. And if you think this is rough, wait until you meet the attorneys for our insurance carrier. It's their money."

I shook my head. We'd been at this for two hours, and I hadn't told half the story.

I was a bear throughout the weekend, and not a cuddly one. Recognizing my mood, Stephanie gave me a wide berth. On Monday, I felt a chill as I entered the newsroom. The paper had not yet reported the lawsuit, but word had seeped across the newsroom floor. It was as though I might be contagious with a grave illness. Everyone felt they should say something, but no one knew what. I went about my work as though nothing had happened, but I was twice pulled into meetings during the week, sessions that took place on the fifth floor, not the fourth. Everyone knew what that meant.

Stephanie avoided me like an apprentice zookeeper, but on the following Wednesday, she called at midafternoon to share news. "I've got it."

"Stephanie Brayman," I said, "Vice President, Manufacturing."

"Senior Vice President," she corrected.

"I am so damned happy for you. Let's run out to Paley's tonight to celebrate."

I made reservations and sat back in my chair, hands clasped behind my neck. Could I now retire and be a kept man, writing my Great American Novel? I would first have to come up with a plot. With characters. I fantasized about that for a few minutes, but was pulled back to reality for another meeting, this with attorneys for the insurance company.

As I entered the conference room, I heard one say, "We're offering to settle."

"Why?" I demanded.

They looked at me as though I were an uninvited guest. Marge introduced me. "Why would we settle?" I repeated. "We've done nothing wrong."

"Because the litigation could cost more than the settlement," one said, "and there's the risk you might lose."

"We should not reward a corrupt public official for criminal actions."

"Look," one said, "this isn't about your ego."

"But it is about my reputation. Mine and the paper's."

"It's academic," Marge said. "We've already asked. Allston's not interested. He wants a show trial."

"Why didn't someone ask me before offering to cave in?" I said.

"It's not all about you. Have I mentioned that?"

I was angry, dispirited, and, by the time the afternoon was over, drained. My spirits did not soar when I arrived at the restaurant to find Mark and Wendy Fisher awaiting a table. Still, I was civil. "I'm meeting Stephanie here. We're celebrating great news she's received."

"I know," Mark said. "She's invited us to join her." The man had an issue with pronouns, but that was the least of my annoyances at the moment. Still, this is who Stephanie wanted to share in her victory dance. The night was hers, and I would not befoul it like the proverbial skunk at a garden party. I behaved myself, letting Stephanie celebrate her achievement.

But through it all, Mark studied me. "How's it going?" he said.

"Fine. Life is busy these days."

"That story two weeks ago about the county commissioner—that was what you were working on?"

"Yes."

"He still got elected."

"That's what the voters decided. It's not up to me."

He prodded a bit more, but I gave away nothing. *He knows. We've published nothing about the lawsuit, the broadcast media hasn't picked it up, but he knows. He's looking at me, studying my reactions, waiting for me to broach the subject.*

No. You're getting paranoid. Get over yourself.

Still, his presence here—and, less so, Wendy's—spoiled the evening. It was as though Stephanie's new position had brought with it a host of new relationships that had nothing to do with us, only with her. I was a bit resentful. More than a bit if I were to admit it.

"When are you coming?" Cheryl called at seven in the morning, ignoring the two-hour time difference.

"Let me call you back. I'm making breakfast." I pulled bacon from the oven and finished stirring scrambled eggs over an almost imperceptible flame, adding sour cream to end the cooking process once clumps formed. With a dash of salt and pepper and one final stir, I set Stephanie's plate before her.

"You seemed subdued last night."

"I thought I had plenty to say."

"Oh, you were nice enough, said some wonderful things about me. I almost believed them."

"You should. I meant every word. I'm proud of you and what you've accomplished. We both know a woman has to outperform a man by a significant margin to achieve what you have."

"Thanks," she said, "but—"

"What?"

"You went quiet midway through dinner."

"I was tired. The lawyers met with me again yesterday. I feel like —" I broke off. There was no point in avoiding it. "Mark knows about the lawsuit, doesn't he?"

Her slight hesitation gave herself away. "I told him. I said you were under a lot of stress and explained why." I played with my breakfast, sulking. "He's our friend, Alan."

"There are things we can share with our friends and things that should be between—" The bleating of our home phone interrupted my response.

I threw my napkin into the congealing plate of eggs and took the phone. "We're having breakfast, Cheryl." I stalked through the house to the home office and slammed the door.

"There's a lot going on here, too. This is no picnic. Hello? Are you still there?"

"Where else would I be?"

"You should be here, in Austin. You promised to come home after the election. You were in Chicago; you could have flown down from there."

"The newspaper summoned me back to Portland on short notice to deal with a business issue."

"You have people working for you. Assign it to a reporter."

"Cheryl, damn it, it's a matter that involves me personally. No one else can handle it."

"You needn't shout."

"Evidently, I do."

"Mother needs us. This situation cannot continue. It's intolerable."

"I promise I'll get there as soon as I can, but it won't be for at least another week, maybe two. This is not within my control."

"Nothing seems to be. When our father left, Mother didn't say, 'I don't have time for you kids. I'm busy now.' She did what she needed to do—"

"I am not prepared to endure another paean to Mother's selflessness. Our conversations always follow a pattern. Father left us alone and penniless, Mother stepped in and did the right thing, and now we owe her."

"Well, that's a fact."

"It's the lede and also all the B-copy."

"What?"

"Never mind. I'll get there as soon as I can. I have to deal with a crisis. If I don't—" I dropped the thought, not wanting to consider or-elses.

I hung up, dressed, and left the house, driving not to work, but to the Japanese Garden where my membership gets me early admission. It was cold this morning, but a few photographers were braving the chilly mists to get beauty shots. None were near my bench at the base of the Natural Garden. I tried chasing all thoughts from my mind— the lawsuit, Stephanie, Cheryl, Mother, the Fishers, everyone and everything.

I struggled for half an hour and gave up. The stock market was plummeting, families were losing their homes and living in cars, businesses were shuttering because they couldn't get credit, and I was sitting on a wooden bench on a cold, damp day feeling sorry for myself. *It's not all about you, Alan.*

Asa Miner had been clear in his instructions. "Don't contact any of the subjects in your story. If they try to reach you, don't speak to them. The court may construe any interaction you have as witness tampering."

It made perfect sense, and I intended to abide by it. With one exception. The documents Weaver had given me were a major issue in the lawsuit. Allston claimed some were doctored and others were fabrications. He claimed his opponent, Nate Pearson, had supplied them, either directly or through a third party.

Only I knew Weaver was my source, and I needed to learn how he had obtained the documents, perhaps even get him to come forward and testify to their authenticity. The problem was how to reach him. I had his phone number but didn't want to risk calling him from my home, office, or cell phone in the event Allston's attorneys subpoenaed my records. The days of strolling down the street to a phone booth were over, but I knew the bus station had a bank of public phones.

Portland's bus terminal lies next to the train station on 6th Avenue, and it's a depressing place. Ranks of homeless adults surrounded the building. A homeless man with blondish hair matted against his scalp leaned against the wall outside the terminal, peeing against the bricks while others ignored him. The first two phone booths were out of order, the receiver ripped from the wall in one of them. A third was in working order, but so stank of urine and defecation I couldn't stand to be in it. The fourth was acceptable. I dialed Weaver's number and deposited the necessary coins. I got no answer, considered leaving a message, but decided against it. *Leave no trace*, I told myself.

I called the airport when I returned to the office and learned there were payphones near the administrative suite. Stephanie was attending an event that evening, so I took light rail into the terminal and called Weaver's number. Again, no answer.

How could I reach him without others knowing? I puzzled over the problem as I rode back into town. I couldn't visit the clerk's office and shouldn't risk even calling there.

When I reached the *Examiner* the following morning, I called Traci Jacobs. "I've been waiting to hear from you," she said. "Any word on that lease? It's only five weeks until the end of the year."

Hell. Weeks before, I'd promised to let her know if I heard anything from legal. "Not a word, Traci. I promise to ask again this afternoon." I too was curious about the hold-up. How long did it take to decide on the future status of the bureaus? "Meanwhile, I need you to do something for me and keep it to yourself. Agreed?"

"Anything that's legal."

I asked her to call the Franklin County Clerk's office and ask to speak to Ralph Weaver. "Identify yourself, assure him you're acting in confidence, and ask him to call me on my cell phone." She had my personal number, but I made her repeat it to be sure. "If he's not there, don't leave a message. Tell them you'll call him back later."

She asked no questions, but I knew she was savvy enough to figure Weaver must be my source. I called Marjorie Cason and asked for the status of Traci's lease. "We haven't decided," she said.

"Look, something's going on. You know it, I know it, and Traci can smell it. I need to level with her."

"Speak to Bartley about it," she said. "It's out of my hands."

I called Bart and put the same question to him. "Hold on a bit longer, Alan. We'll announce our plans in December."

"Announce what?"

"I can't say at the moment. We're making changes, and we don't want word leaking out before we have all the pieces in place. By the way, *Portland Weekly* knows about the libel suit. I just got off the phone with them. They're running a story tomorrow. You'd better rehearse your 'no comment.'"

I thanked him for the alert and placed the handset back in its cradle in time for the phone to ring. I answered with my usual greeting.

"This is Josh Zydell." Josh was the top reporter at the city's alternative news weekly. We were friendly competitors, and I respected him.

"Let me make this easy by being difficult. I can't comment on Allston's lawsuit." He posed several more questions, asking for responses to allegations taken from the filing. I held my ground as he knew I would.

"Off the record?" I asked. He paused before agreeing. "I would love nothing more than to unload—about my story, about Allston, and about the process. But I'm under orders not to. If you were in my shoes, you'd face the same constraints."

"I know," he said. "Good luck."

I tried to work on my next column but couldn't concentrate. I did the electronic equivalent of paper shuffling for a while, forced myself to finish the column, and grabbed a sandwich for lunch. As I sat at my desk, my cell phone chimed.

"I have bad news," said Traci. Sometimes I imagine I can feel my blood pressure changing. I did so now. "I called over there, and a woman told me he's no longer with the clerk's office. I asked how I could reach him. She didn't want to speak, began sobbing, and hung up. I knew from her reaction something had happened, so I called around—the local hospital, funeral homes."

"And?"

"Ralph Weaver was found dead in his home two weeks ago with a gunshot wound to his head. They're treating it as a suicide." I was stunned into silence. "Does that seem right? Would he do something like that?"

"It's possible. He was nervous. But I don't think so."

"He was your guy, wasn't he?"

"Traci, I can't comment on that. But thanks."

I sat at my desk for some time, how long I can't say. I left the office, walked up Burnside to 23rd Street, up Park Avenue towards the Japanese Garden.

Stephanie and I had seen little of each other for a week, so consumed was she in her new responsibilities. Over breakfast one morning, I asked her what she'd decided about joining the symphony board.

"Oh, that's off," she said. "Rebecca Johnston, our VP of Community Affairs, wants me to get involved with something involving young people."

"Oh," I said as though it were a novel idea.

"She's reached out to New Horizons for Youth. It's a mentorship program for African American youngsters. She's asked them to consider me for the board and offered a sponsorship package. It's a win-win."

"That's great."

"You don't sound enthusiastic."

I put down my newspaper. "I am. It's the sort of thing I hoped you'd latch onto. I'm glad you followed your heart."

"It was Rebecca's suggestion. Victor has no interest in classical music."

But if I thought this switch was about to rid me of one of the more annoying individuals Steph had dragged into our lives, I was mistaken. "Mark is fine with it. I think he's losing interest in the symphony."

Under my questioning, she divulged that the board has passed him over for a term as chairman in favor of a member who had served since Brahms' mother lullabied him to sleep. Wendy had nailed that one.

"He's somewhat peripatetic," I said. She gave me a quizzical look, but I didn't elaborate.

"He's invited us for Thanksgiving dinner. It will save you from having to mess around in the kitchen all day."

I felt no need to be saved and would have appreciated being asked. I had hoped to get together with a couple of old friends we hadn't seen in months, but Steph had been noncommittal about my plan and went ahead and made one of her own.

On Thanksgiving Day, we arrived at the Fishers' home in Lake Oswego armed with two bottles of Oregon pinot noir. Wendy greeted us at the door, took our coats, and carried the wine into the kitchen. Mark introduced us to another couple, David and Roxanne Galloway, who lived nearby.

Galloway was in something called reinsurance. He tried to explain it, but I lost interest about the time he went into the intricacies of corporate self-insurance and interrogated me about how the *Examiner* handled its health, general liability, and errors and omissions coverage. I said I didn't know since I was on the editorial, not the business side. He gave me his card and asked me to forward it to those in the business office. I promised to do so, a white lie.

As we sat down to Wendy's dinner, Mark said, "I read in *PW* that you're being sued."

"Yes, a politician in Eastern Oregon claims we libeled him with a story we did."

"Isn't that the one you were working on?"

"Yes. I'm not at liberty to discuss it. Attorneys, you know."

"What are his chances?"

"I can't comment on this case, but it's difficult for a public official to prove libel against a news outlet. They must not only prove the story was wrong, but that the reporter knew it was wrong, and that he wrote it out of malice."

"So it would be terrible if you lost."

"Mark," Stephanie said, "Alan cannot discuss the case." Before I could give her a mental high five, she added, "But it's worrisome." I was ready to leave the table and drive to the Turkey Place, a Portland restaurant on Southwest Second Avenue that serves—you guessed it —turkey every day of the year.

"This wine is outstanding," Galloway said. He too seemed to know this was the only way to get Mark to change the subject.

"It's a Walla Walla syrah. Wendy and I have a relationship with this winery. We go out there every May and collect several cases. I find it goes well with poultry."

The pinot noir had disappeared somewhere, never to appear at the Fishers' Thanksgiving table. Mark was wrong. The syrah over-powered the turkey, masking its flavors with a frontal assault of fruit and alcohol. I decided Mark was being provocative, annoying me and hoping to get a reaction. He didn't succeed. I retreated from the conversation and, when it was time to clear the table, manned the sink and dishwasher over Wendy's objections.

She gave me a hug as we worked, perhaps in gratitude for not engaging Mark in his little games.

"What did you think?" Stephanie said as I drove back into town.

"What do you think I think?"

She didn't answer, and we had little more to say to each other as we ended a day for which I had little to be thankful, save that it was over.

Working through a contact in Franklin County to avoid involving the paper, Traci obtained a copy of both the police and the medical examiner's reports on Ralph Weaver's death. His mother had become concerned two weekends before when he didn't show up to take her to church and didn't answer her phone call. She'd called a neighbor and asked her to check on him. The neighbor had found the door unlocked, which was not unusual in a small town like Center City, and, on entering the kitchen, had seen Weaver lying in a pool of dried blood. She'd backed out, returned to her home, and called the police department.

The examining officer found a .38 Special lying next to Weaver on the kitchen floor. One chamber was empty. Weaver's prints were the only ones on the weapon. There was no note, no sign of forced entry, no sign of a struggle, and the toxicology report indicated no drug or alcohol use.

The medical examiner recovered a bullet that had entered Weaver's brain through his right temple. Weaver was right-handed. The bullet matched a test round fired from the weapon. The medical examiner determined he had last eaten several hours before his death and fixed the time of death at between 4:00 and 6:00 on the previous Saturday afternoon. The death was ruled a suicide. There was no evidentiary reason I could see to rule otherwise.

Traci spoke with a neighbor who said Weaver's mother was distraught and could not believe her son had taken his own life. She had talked with him only hours before and said he had seemed cheerful because he had been offered a job opportunity. His last words to her were, "I'll pick you up at 10:30, Ma. We'll go to church. Then I'll take you to lunch."

She did not accept the official cause of death, and, remembering the concern Weaver had expressed for his mother at our meeting, neither did I. But our attorneys insisted I did no digging in Franklin County while the suit was being litigated, and I wouldn't have known where to start.

For years, Stephanie and I spent the Sunday after Thanksgiving visiting Willamette Valley wineries, most of which throw their doors open on this weekend. As I studied the wine map in the special section of the *Examiner*, however, Stephanie begged off. "We need to talk," she said.

After I'd cleared the breakfast dishes, we sat across from each other in the living room. I was ready for a discussion about Mark Fisher, perhaps even an apology for her subjecting me to his behavior, but I got something else entirely.

"We're worried about the libel suit," she said.

"Who is 'we'?"

"The attorneys at Victor." Before I could ask what interest they had in the case, she said, "I'm in a different position now than when we married—different even from a month ago. I'm making substantially more money, and I'm an officer of a company with an international reputation."

"I don't see how Brill Allston's trying to exact revenge has anything to do with Victor Apparel."

"To them, it's a matter of reputational risk. There's also the risk that my assets could become entwined with yours if the judgment goes against you."

"First, Allston will not win this lawsuit." I spoke with more confidence than I felt. Our attorneys were pummeling me with questions that made me feel guilty. The only person who could have validated the documents we'd printed was dead. "I suppose there's a chance he could get a judgment in a lower court, but in that event, we would appeal and carry it all the way to the Supreme Court, if necessary. All the precedents are on our side."

"We can't take that chance."

"You'd better tell me what you want."

She rose and walked into the family room, brought back her attaché case, and extracted a long gray envelope. "This is what's called an antenuptial agreement. It's like a prenuptial, but it's an agreement made after a marriage rather than before it. It separates a couple's assets and earnings, so that what affects one party doesn't affect the other. It's commonplace in situations like this."

"You want a divorce," I said.

"No. I knew you'd react this way." She held her head in her hands.

"How am I supposed to react? For twenty-five years, we have supported each other's personal goals and careers. Now you're saying, 'I've had a change in status, and I don't want to share anything with you.'"

"It's not about money!" She shook her head. "Not *only* about money. You're making this so difficult."

"What is it about, Stephanie, if not money?"

"It's about—" She flailed for the right words. "It protects me and the position I've achieved in the event that you lose this case."

I said nothing. "It doesn't affect our relationship or our marriage. I still love you. We still have our family—Eric—what we've built. It's a firewall against whatever may happen in the future. And it protects you, too. What if I do something wrong and am sued for it?"

"So you think I've done something wrong."

She stood up and almost threw the document at me. "Stop taking this personally. Read the thing. Discuss it with a lawyer. But please, *please* sign it. Out of respect for your wife."

I took it without another word, left the house, and didn't return until Tuesday night, at which point Stephanie was on a flight over the Pacific to inspect her factories in China.

CHAPTER SIX
DECEMBER 2008

Allston had filed his lawsuit in Franklin County. Doons Bradberry petitioned for a change of venue, arguing that the *Examiner* could not get a fair trial there. On the first day of December, the judge gave Allston an early Christmas present by denying our motion. We would face trial in a county that had just voted Brill Allston into the Oregon Senate by a 3-1 margin.

The unlikelihood of getting a fair trial was only one reason for my gloom this morning. I sat in Bart's office and, after getting his pledge of silence, told him my news. "My source is gone. He died two weekends ago of a gunshot wound. The official report is that it was self-inflicted, but I don't believe it."

"I hope you're not accusing Allston of murder." I thought for a moment and then shook my head. "We need to let Marjorie in on this."

I protested, but Townes was insistent. Marge came in, listened without taking notes, and then said, "How do you know this?"

"I tried to reach him and, when I couldn't, had a third party check for me."

"Who is this third party?"

"What difference does it make?"

"We told you not to speak with witnesses."

"A, this source would never have been a witness, because I was unwilling to reveal the name. B, I did not tell the third party why I was trying to reach this individual."

She leaned toward me and said, "Can we please cut the crap? Who did the checking for you?"

Bartley Townes nodded his insistence.

"Traci Jacobs."

She sighed and shook her head. "You've involved another reporter in this mess. I'm not happy about that. She's a smart lady and probably guessed why you were using her."

She had, but I didn't admit it. "If Allston discovers she was asking questions about your source, he'll have her subpoenaed, and she'll be in the same position you are. Although," she said, "I don't know what difference it makes, now that your source is dead."

"Alan thinks the death is suspicious," Townes said.

I presented my reasoning—Weaver's concern for his mother and his promise made only hours before his death to take her to church and to lunch the following day. "I know it's circumstantial and that my source was a nervous nelly, but this doesn't seem the actions of a person about to commit suicide."

"You can stop playing with pronouns," she said. "There can't be that many suicides within a 48-hour period in Franklin County. I'll have his name in a matter of minutes. If I want it. Which I don't."

She stood up in a gesture of dismissal. "I have to leave town for a few days," I said. "My mother needs me."

Marge and Bart exchanged glances. "That might be a good thing," she said. "It'll keep you from doing more harm while we work on a few more motions."

When I left Austin years ago, I couldn't afford the airfare to Oregon, so I drove there in a third-hand, decade-old Honda Civic with a single suitcase and two boxes of books in the back. Had I flown, I would have left from a dinky little airport close in on the east side, unbefitting of the capital of the fastest-growing state in the nation.

What I returned to now was a bustling international airport created out of the shuttered Bergstrom Air Force Base, which Air Force One had used during Lyndon Johnson's presidency. Though it was just past lunchtime, traffic clogged I-35 as I drove north to Cheryl's home. Austin seemed like a fat child who had busted out of his clothing but whose parents were too stingy to buy new ones. It sprawled in all directions, invading the Texas Hill Country like an army of grasshoppers, devouring everything in its path. Yet in its heart, it remained Austin—Waylon, Willie, and Gary P. Nunn, Pecan Street, Barton Springs, and Longhorn football.

Halfway up MoPac Boulevard, I changed my plan, exited east on Guadalupe north of the university, and parked in front of Mother's small bungalow, a place she couldn't afford were she to buy it today.

"Hi, Sonny," she said. She knows I hate that name. "Where's your sister?"

"I came to see you first."

"I'll call and let her know you're here."

"There's time for that," I said. "Let's talk, just the two of us."

"Oh, I know how she likes to hog the conversation. This'll be fine."

I asked how she was doing. "My CPAP machine is broken, and they won't fix it. Plus, we've had so much rain, Arthur Itis is paying me a visit."

"Old Arthur." We chuckled over the familiar family joke. She walked into the kitchen and returned with a glass of iced tea. "I knew you were coming, so I made it unsweetened."

I thanked her. Despite Old Arthur, she moved well, a slight favoring of her left side but nothing that most people would have noticed unless they were looking for it.

"What's this about a broken machine?"

"CPAP. It helps me breathe at night. I have sleep hernia." It took me a moment to translate this into sleep apnea. "The mask is broken, and they won't send me another."

"Who's 'they?'"

"The company. Medicare won't pay for it because I haven't been using the machine. I'm not sure how they know that, but they do."

I thumbed through the instruction manual and found that the instrument sent a daily report of how many hours it had been in use. Since the connection between the hose and mask had split, it leaked air and didn't function. "Did you explain to them why it doesn't work?"

"Yes, but they won't send me another because Medicare won't approve it. They say I don't qualify for a replacement since I don't use it."

I looked up the part and ordered it online. We made small talk. She told a story about a woman named Evans. "Gladys Evans," she said. "You remember."

"No, I don't believe I do."

"Sure you do. She used to live next door, she and her husband, Carl. He was a ne'er-do-well, never worked a lick in his life."

"The Bartlesons lived next door when I was here."

"The other side."

"Sorry, I don't remember them. I left in '81, remember."

"They lived here long before that, I'm sure of it. Give me the phone, I'll ask Cheryl."

"Mom, it makes no difference. Tell me the story."

She sat for a moment. "I can't remember now. Isn't that funny? It happens all the time."

My cell phone chimed to save me from telling her that maybe it wasn't that important to begin with. "Where are you?" Cheryl demanded. "Your flight landed more than an hour ago."

"I'm with Mother. We were about to call you."

"That is so rude."

"You can bless me out when you get here," I said, winking at Mother, whose grin showed she was enjoying the family drama.

"I want you to promise me something, Sonny," she said once Cheryl ended the call.

"Only if you call me Alan."

"Your father insisted on that name, have I ever mentioned that?" She had, many times. "I wanted to name you after him, but he wanted you to have your own name." She sniffed. "Only unselfish thing he ever did. Running off like that when you were a little boy, leaving us all alone. How I struggled." She emitted a long sigh.

"What were you about to ask me, Mom?"

"Don't let her do it. She wants to move me to an old folks' home. I don't want to go. I have my little house here, and my friends. I'm doing fine on my own. I don't want a bunch of strangers pushing me around, telling me what to do."

It was the same conversation as the previous month. She made the same arguments. I gave the same responses. We got nowhere. "Promise me," she said.

"Mom, I can't do that. I promise to do nothing that's not in your best interests, and I won't force anything on you. We need to hear Cheryl out. She's the one who looks after you."

"I can look after myself." Tears came to her eyes, and she did not hide them.

I can't stand to see Mother cry. I retreated to the kitchen to make her a cup of tea. Cheryl's arrival came as a relief. "What have you done to upset her?" she demanded.

"Nothing. We're just talking."

"You need to watch what you say around her. Her emotions are right on the surface. The least little thing—"

"Stop talking about me as though I'm not here."

"All right, Mother. See, Alan? This is why I asked you to come to my place first."

"I wanted to spend a few minutes alone with her."

"Well, you see what happened."

I endured more back-and-forth, Mother remembering the story of Gladys Evans. "Alan says he doesn't remember her."

"He wouldn't," she said. "They moved here in 1982. Alan had already left for Oregon." She mispronounced it, stressing the final syllable. In years past, I would correct her whenever she did it. I finally gave up, concluding that it was deliberate, her way of needling me for leaving them.

"Willamette," I said. They looked at me in confusion. "That's the river flowing through Portland. Many people say Will-a-METT, but it's Will-AM-it, damn it."

"Don't be such a smart ass," Cheryl said. She stood up, gathering her authority around her. "Are we ready to go?"

"Go where?" Mother said.

"To Barton Creek. We're looking at an apartment there. That's why Alan has come all this way."

This was news to both of us. "I don't think Mother is ready—"

"Damn you! I've made all the arrangements. Don't interfere. Mother, get your things. You will love this place."

We bundled into her car, Mother sitting up front alongside Cheryl while I sprawled across the back seat.

The retirement home was a four-story building behind a curving driveway. We entered an atrium framed by a long glass window that overlooked a swimming pool, closed at this time of the year but inviting in Austin's hot summer weather. No one occupied the brightly colored sofas and chairs placed around the room. I wondered if the managers had shooed away the residents with company coming. Then again, it was mid-afternoon. Perhaps everyone was taking a nap.

A tall, dark-haired woman greeted us, introducing herself as Elena Garza. She wore a clingy dress in a silvery fabric and open-toed shoes with three-inch heels, the variety that Stephanie called calf-killers when forced to wear them. Ms. Garza gave Mother a broad smile and led us into a room where a video was on pause. After a few introductory remarks, she played the presentation, which showed good-looking, healthy men and women I judged to be a few years shy of retirement age enjoying tennis, swimming, playing cards, eating, and, through it all, laughing. The female narrator spoke in a deep alto voice that had never known a shout. As the video ended, the camera did a 180 around a table at which two couples were seated, zooming in on one of the quartet, an attractive woman with salt and pepper hair. She was the spokesperson to whom we'd been listening for the past six minutes. It was all uptown, professional, and persuasive.

As the video faded to black, my mother turned to Ms. Garza and said, "I don't have a husband. This wouldn't be that much fun for me."

She emitted a practiced laugh. "Many widows find companions here."

"I'm not a widow. I'm divorced. My husband left me years ago, me and these kids."

Cheryl sighed. "C'mon, Mom, let's take a tour."

The saleswoman—for that's what Ms. Garza was—led us into the dining room where round tables set for six filled the space, each covered with a beige linen tablecloth. Large photos of the Texas Hill Country, bursting with color from wildflowers, lined two long walls.

She led us upstairs and into a room that served as the library. Women much older than those in the video looked up from their books but didn't speak. Two walkers rested near the room's entrance.

The atmosphere was livelier in the third-floor game room. Players filled eight tables—some engaged in mahjong, others in bridge, and one group playing a spirited game of something they called spite and malice. Their angry comments to each other reflected the name.

"You remember," Mother said. "We used to play that years ago." I didn't but said I did.

"You'd enjoy this," Cheryl said. "Think of all the fun you could have playing that game."

"I don't play cards anymore," Mother said.

Ms. Garza showed a model two-bedroom apartment with modern furnishings which reflected the facility's preference for bold, primary colors. A high-definition television set hung over a gas fireplace that pumped heat into the room. The kitchenette was so well stocked, there was no counter space left to prep food. "Most of our residents only make lunch," she said when I raised the point. "We provide three meals a day, and the guests may choose which two they come down for. They can also purchase all three if they wish."

"I don't get up for breakfast," Mother said.

"And we also have one-bedroom apartments for singles."

"I'd need a two-bedroom," Mother said, "for when Alan comes to visit." I rolled my eyes at Cheryl, who ignored me.

"What did you think?" I asked Mother when we'd returned to her house.

"It's nice, but I could never live there. It's too small for me. Too regimented."

I said it did not seem so, but Mother said it did, and that settled it.

"Here's an option. Stephanie and I have been exploring apartments in Portland—not retirement homes, but apartments for seniors." I suspect they were little different from what we'd just toured, having not visited any, but I tried to differentiate them. "What would you think of moving to Oregon? It's a beautiful place to live."

Cheryl glared at me. I mouthed the words, "What's wrong?"

She motioned me into the dining room. "I can't believe you're suggesting that."

"I thought you wanted—"

"I have devoted my life to my mother. You will not take her away from me."

"I'm only trying to help."

"Besides, she hates rain, and she couldn't stand to be around that wife of yours."

"Fine," I said. "Have it your way. But you can work it out with her."

"Some help you are, springing that on her."

"Like you sprung the tour of this facility on both of us?"

"That was why I brought you here, to support me in this decision."

I sat in silence for the rest of the afternoon. Cheryl was right about one thing. Not once had Mother asked about Stephanie.

"This is a Come to Jesus moment," Asa Miner said. I wanted to crack that I'm not religious and that he was calling on the wrong deity, but sensed that this might not be the right moment. I rotated my coffee mug with my fingers and settled back to listen.

"Oregon's shield law protects reporters from having to reveal their sources or disclose their notes. It's broad, extending to interviews not included in a story and even to conversations in which the reporter hasn't promised confidentiality. But there are three important exceptions, one of which applies to our case."

McAllister took over for him. "In a defamation case, if the defense seeks to prove the accuracy of a story using information provided by an informant, it must reveal his identity. Allston's attorney has moved that the judge force you to do so. We're arguing that, while your original information came from a confidential source, you verified everything through other sources before publication."

I nodded in agreement.

"But they counter that the documents we printed have been altered and, in one case, forged. That's the bill of sale for the beef. They demand that we reveal who supplied them. We don't know how this will turn out, but, as your attorneys, we need to know the source."

I looked to Marge for guidance but got none.

"The shield law does not apply here," Asa Miner said. "The court can order you to reveal his name. If you refuse, the judge can hold you in contempt and send you to prison, none of the documents your source provided will be admitted into evidence, *and we will lose this case.*"

"I've never revealed a confidential source," I said. "I need to think about this."

"You do that."

The period between Thanksgiving and Christmas should be the happiest time of the year, but those who feel lonely dread it. My father left us during those weeks in 1967. Years later, my college love, Jeanie, left me on Christmas Eve. I have always approached the holidays with trepidation, and I regard any setback that occurs in December as the fulfillment of prophecy.

The lawsuit, the tug-of-war with Cheryl over Mother's future, and Stephanie's demand for what I persisted in calling a prenup combined to make 2008 one of the lowest years of my life. The irony was that, with the election of the nation's first African-American president, those around me seemed buoyant, even many who hadn't voted for him. There was something new and vibrant in the air, but I wasn't a part of it.

Stephanie had flown from Shanghai to Hanoi during the week, and I was still alone in the house. I seldom drink, apart from the occasional glass of wine. It might have helped if I did. I moped around the house, staying up late reading or watching old movies.

As news of the lawsuit became public, the temperature at the *Examiner* turned frosty. Colleagues didn't speak without purpose; they didn't know what to say. I lumbered through the newsroom like a bear in hibernation, scarcely hearing the questions from the reporters and columnists who report to me. Every day followed a pattern—up to the conference room and back to my desk, where I got little accomplished.

Two days before Stephanie's return, I decided to preempt whatever her plan for the holiday might be. I called our son, Eric, whom I hadn't heard from in weeks. We exchanged pleasantries. I inquired as to his studies and his hunt for a post-graduation job. "We haven't talked about your plans for Christmas, but I hope you'll be coming home."

His hesitation told me he wouldn't. "I already talked to Mom about that. I'm spending it with Keiko's family in San Francisco."

"I didn't know. Is there any chance you could shift things around? I'd like to see you—both of you."

"Dad, I've promised. We've planned this for weeks. I can't..."

"Sure. I get it. You're serious, then?"

"Me and Keiko?"

I cringed, wanting to say, 'Keiko and I.'

"Yeah, we're—uh—together."

"I'm glad someone has it together."

"What? What's wrong?"

"Nothing. You know how I enjoy wordplay. Everything's fine."

"Mom says you're fighting some kind of lawsuit."

I told him about it, and for once he focused. "Will you be all right?"

"Oh, sure. We're covered. It won't affect us personally."

"Mom is worried about that."

"I know." I explained the process, expressing confidence we would win outright and that, failing that, we would prevail on appeal. We wished each other Merry Christmas and said our goodbyes. I thought for several minutes about how to fight off another bout of Fisher-itis, then called around in Cannon Beach until I found a room for the holiday weekend. I booked it, paying in advance. I bought a tree, hauled our stand and ornaments down from the attic room above the garage, and decorated it, knowing Stephanie would move every-thing around when she returned.

For weeks, I'd detected an undercurrent of something pulling at the editorial side of the newspaper. I was certain Bartley Townes knew something he wasn't telling the editors. Or was I overreacting to

Allston's lawsuit? On the day Stephanie returned, I got my answer. Bart walked into the newsroom minutes after the deadline and called together all the editors and supervisors.

"As you know, newspapers throughout the country are struggling," he said. "The Internet has undermined our classified ad revenue, the economy is taking out traditional advertisers, and newsprint costs are skyrocketing. The *Examiner* is an independent newspaper, and because we're a local institution, the board has fought against making cuts as long as they can. This has been a brutal year. We will finish with a $2 million loss."

He paused and looked around the room. "We must make cuts. They involve more than personnel; they go to the heart of who we are." The *Examiner* would stop trying to be a statewide newspaper. It was ending circulation in Eastern Oregon, the Coast, and south of Albany. It would close bureaus in those areas, reduce its Capitol Bureau by half, and reduce editorial staff in Portland by 20 percent.

"We'll be working through this over the next few weeks," he said. "Some reductions will be through attrition and some though early retirement buy-outs. We hope that will be enough." Attrition? That implied that some of us would choose to leave during a deepening recession. Who was he kidding? We all looked at each other, wondering who would no longer be sitting next to us in two weeks' time. Or whether we might be among those looking for a chair.

I waited fifteen minutes before knocking at his door. "Eastern Oregon, the Capitol—those are my staff members. Who tells them?"

"We'll brief you in the morning. We'll have severance information ready for each employee, and then you'll have time to call them."

"Not good enough. You think Traci and the crew in Salem won't have heard about this within the hour?"

I realized I was shouting at the man. The thin band that had held me together for the past few weeks was about to snap.

"You'll do as you're damned well told," he growled, "or you can leave with them. Your choice!"

I picked Stephanie up at the airport an hour later, despite her insistence she'd take a cab. I listened to her foreign adventures, which she stripped of any detail that might be useful to a journalist, then told her about the looming cutbacks at the paper.

"Are you worried?"

"No. Not yet, anyway. I'm angry. It's the week before Christmas. They've known this was coming for months. They're ruining people's lives at the holidays."

"Would they have felt better if it had come the week before Thanksgiving?"

I couldn't argue with the logic. "In your absence, I decided something on our behalf."

"You're signing the agreement?" she said.

"No, I'm still thinking about that. I'm meeting with an attorney tomorrow. No, this is about Christmas. Eric is spending the week with his girlfriend—"

"I thought we'd invite the Fishers over. We owe them."

"No," I said. "We're going to the Coast, just the two of us. We'll sit by a fire, watch the waves, sample all the restaurants in Cannon Beach, go up to Astoria and dine at that little restaurant over the Columbia River—do the things we did when we were first married."

"Shouldn't we discuss this?" she said.

"It's a surprise. One of my Christmas gifts. I've already paid for it." Two of us could be peremptory. I assured her she'd have a good time, but, given her reaction, I wasn't so sure.

The following morning, six of us gathered in the fifth-floor conference room while Tisha Gregory, the HR director, and Marjorie Cason handed us folders containing the names of those to be sacrificed to the god of profits, and led us through what we could and could not say. Gregory told us we were likely to encounter pleas, tears, and anger, but were to remain firm. She offered to sit in on conversations with anyone who felt uncomfortable in this role. Three of the six raised their hands.

"How about you, Alan?"

I assured her I could manage, but wondered why she hadn't asked the remaining two. The Capitol bureau was the most complex, since I needed to include Nadine Walker, the bureau chief, in the discussion. I wouldn't do this on the phone; I had to handle it in person. I called Nadine and asked that she keep the three reporters in the office until I arrived.

I met with her first in our small bureau four blocks from the Capitol. One of the two being terminated was a young reporter who had not yet found his feet and didn't seem likely to. He was taking so much of Nadine's time, it affected her productivity, so she was not sorry to lose him. The other, however, was a rising star, someone Nadine had hoped would replace her as she headed toward retirement.

"Why didn't they buy me out?" she asked. I told her I didn't know, which was true, though I suspected they planned to reduce the bureau to one reporter once she left the paper.

The meeting went better than I'd expected. Because Nadine had asked them to stay in the office, both had a sense of what was coming. The young reporter seemed relieved, as though he knew he wasn't performing and was glad to end the suspense. The budding star took it in stride, asking the right questions about severance, vacation pay, and health insurance, then wishing us well.

"That was a strange reaction," I said when they'd left, referring to the rising star.

"I suspect he already has something lined up. He's no fool. He may have known this was coming before we did." The accuracy of her appraisal became clear two weeks later when, on the first workday of 2009, the state's public broadcasting network announced he was joining them.

Nadine and I had lunch. I used her office to call Traci. "How long have you known this?" she said when I'd finished my script.

"They told me last night, but I wasn't free to inform you until they gave me the details on severance this morning."

"But how long have you *known*? I asked you to check on the lease over two months go. You must have suspected something then."

"Traci, I didn't. They told me only that they were considering what to do about physical arrangements for the bureaus."

"And you didn't tell me."

"They instructed me not to." This was the type of conversation Tisha and Marge had warned me to avoid.

"You had me do all that checking on Ralph Weaver. You knew I wouldn't be here, but you let me do your dirty work for you."

I wanted to tell her she had it wrong and warn her not to burn her bridges, but she was young and angry, and I sensed that anything I said would only intensify her fury. I ended the conversation as gracefully as I could, told her I regretted we would no longer be working together, and wished her well.

She responded with a two-word epithet that left no doubt how she felt, towards the paper and towards me. In a way, I didn't blame her. Where was she to find another reporting job in Eastern Oregon?

I returned to Portland. I had a late-afternoon meeting with my attorney.

"You're off the hook," Asa Miner said in a phone call the following morning.

"Which hook?" I asked.

"It's the strangest thing. I was about to go another round with you over the identity of your source. I checked the file to see precisely how the motion read and to see if I could find a way around it. I was surprised to find they've dropped the demand."

"When did they do this?" I asked.

"Last Friday. No one noticed it, and if I hadn't checked, I wouldn't have known either. It's odd."

"Not at all," I said. "They no longer need me to reveal the source. They already know."

I wondered how they'd found out and what role their knowledge had played in Weaver's death.

Even if you've never heard of Cannon Beach, you know it. The small seaside community on Oregon's North Coast is a major tourist destination in every month of the year. Ecola State Park affords a sweeping view of the coastline, and you've seen it in films such as *Goonies* and *Kindergarten Cop*. South of town, Haystack Rock towers above the coast, accessible at low tide; it's featured in dozens of car commercials and ads for prescription medications. Every Memorial Day, one of the TV networks does a story on the community's sand castle competition.

The sole source of income is tourism. Galleries, specialty stores, and restaurants line Hemlock Street—it's not just the city's main drag, but its only drag. Visitors comb the shore from spring through fall and come in winter to sit by fireplaces in their hotel rooms while they watch storms roar ashore.

It's a town where you can shut your mental doors against the outside world and enjoy a few days of tranquility—if you can find a parking spot. Steph sulked all the way out US 26, but once we checked into our suite in an oceanfront lodge, she loosened up and began enjoying herself.

She'd brought a computer and packed her attaché case with files, but I urged her to set them aside. "Let's enjoy ourselves for a few days. You've earned this, and I need it."

We ate dinner at a small bistro at the north end of town, dining on roast duck and salmon while a Spanish guitarist played English carols in a corner two tables away. We held hands, expressed our affection for each other, returned to the lodge, and made love. It had been weeks, and with the ocean roaring beneath our oceanfront window, it was a night to remember.

The next morning, we had breakfast in the hotel and opened presents. She'd bought me a watercolor of a river and waterfall while she was in China; I'd purchased a dress she'd spotted in a window in Chicago and a new leather attaché case to replace her battle-scarred one. "I have something else for you," I said, "but it will have to wait until tonight."

At dusk, I drove the twenty miles north to Astoria, where Lewis and Clark had spent their winter two centuries before. I'd picked a restaurant that sits on pilings over the Columbia River. The place was jammed, but we were fortunate to get a table alongside the window where we watched freighters at anchor as they awaited a berth upriver at Portland's Swan Island to unload autos, computer gear, and clothing destined for Victor Apparel's outlets.

The restaurant specialized in Alaskan halibut coated in, of all things, ground coffee. We enjoyed it with a bottle of Oregon chardonnay from vineyards on the Washington side of the Columbia, 120 miles inland.

Over dessert, I said, "I love you."

"And I love you," she said.

"And I trust you." She frowned, not sure where this was headed. "I trust you, and that's why I'm giving you something else for Christmas—something you want."

I took a sealed envelope from the pocket of my pea coat and handed it to her. She opened it. Inside were two copies of the antenuptial agreement.

"Thank you," she said, with tears in her eyes.

I prayed I'd done the right thing.

We extended our stay through the weekend, walking hand in hand on the beach when the wind wasn't blowing, driving south to

Manzanita to another quaint restaurant we'd frequented when we first married, and spending a lot of time in bed. During our free moments, we discussed the agreement. "This means that if I want something and have the money to purchase it, I can do so," I said.

"I suppose so. We're sharing housing and living expenses, paying for our own vehicles, and what's left is ours to do with as we please."

"And that extends to retirement funds," I said.

"I guess so, but why?"

I told her what I had in mind, and for the next three days, we prowled the North Coast from Manzanita north to Sunset Beach. On Sunday, I found what I was after: a two-bedroom oceanfront condominium in Gearhart that a Seattle couple was offering in a distress sale. I made an offer and put down a deposit, drawing on my retirement funds for a hefty down payment. I hoped that a gullible lender would approve me for the rest in this debt-restricted environment. It would be a place we would enjoy together but that I could call my own when Stephanie was off on one of her trips and I needed a refuge from the pressure of work.

I made another concession that weekend, agreeing to host the Fishers and Galloways for New Year's Eve. In return, I got to invite Bartley Townes and his wife, and another newsroom colleague. Neither accepted, both citing prior commitments. My growing paranoia suggested I was damaged goods, and no one wanted my company. That made the evening even harder to take.

Mark and Wendy arrived first, Mark bearing two bottles of champagne-style wine from California. I had purchased French Champagne at considerable expense, but shrugged it off, figuring there would come a time to share the good stuff with more appreciative company.

I'd prepared Tuscan pork loin with winter root vegetables, pairing it with two bottles of Umbrian wine I'd discovered in a local restaurant. Mark told us how he much preferred the reds from "Piemonte." I ignored him, but Wendy rolled her eyes and grinned at me.

He and Roxanne flanked Steph at one end of the table while David and Wendy sat next to me. Mark and Steph became so engaged in conversation that Roxanne tuned in to ours. Our group talked about the new president and our hope for the next year. David had little of the latter due to his low opinion of the former.

At midnight, we toasted the New Year with Mark's bubbly. Steph and I shared a kiss while Mark and Wendy merely hugged each other.

Weeks later, I ran into Paul Scoby, who, along with his wife, Polly, had been our friends for years. "We missed you New Year's Eve," he said. I apologized and mumbled an excuse, hiding the fact I was unaware they had invited us. Stephanie was sloughing off our old friends like a molting snake shedding its skin.

A *llston v. Oregon Examiner* was to go to trial on the second floor of the Franklin County Courthouse. We encamped in Central City on the first Monday in January, setting up shop in the same Best Western where I'd stayed in August.

We'd spent the three days after New Year's in the Doons Bradberry conference room as the two attorneys took me through my story, coaching me on what to say and, more importantly, what not to say. As a reporter, simple yes or no answers annoyed me, forcing me to probe to unearth whatever my source knew. When asked a question, my impulse was to answer it fully. Miner and McAllister coached me to be less forthcoming, to answer only what I was asked and volunteer nothing. I had also grown accustomed to the contentious nature of the questions. "Haven't you always had it in for Senator Allston?"

"No, I don't believe I'd met the man before I sought him out in October."

"Just 'No,'" McAllister reminded me.

"No."

"Do you recall a statewide conference of county commissioners in Portland in 2006?"

"No."

"You covered it. Your byline is on the article."

"I cover many stories. I don't recall this."

He handed me the photostat of an article, encased in a plastic sheet. "Is this your story?"

I looked it over and recalled the event. "Yes."

"Read the fifth paragraph."

"'Brill Allston, chairman of the Franklin County Commission, spent over a quarter-hour questioning the state highway commission about the allocation of funds for county roads in rural areas. When he refused to yield the floor, fellow commissioners shouted at him until he did so.'"

"Do you still maintain you never met him?"

"Yes," I said. "I covered that meeting, but I never met Allston. He made a fool of himself that day. Other commissioners were furious with him."

"We don't need the editorial comment," Miner said. "It will get you into trouble."

The *Examiner* and I had a choice. We could have the circuit judge decide our fate or opt for a jury trial. The Doons Bradberry attorneys had examined past decisions by Judge Bernie Yates and sensed he harbored considerable hostility to the press and to Portland's dominance of state politics, a view reinforced by the speed with which he had denied our motion for a change of venue. They recommended we take our chances with a jury.

It made sense, but the night before jury selection was to begin, a man approached our table at dinner, looked at me, and said, "You're going to jail."

"And from this worthy stock, we're selecting our jury," I said.

As hot as the courthouse was in summer, it was frigid in winter. Franklin County needed to level the place and start over. The demolition contract alone would have presented abundant opportunity for graft.

But it was too late for that. We entered the courtroom on

Tuesday morning in business suits, noting that everyone else sported thermal vests. It took an hour for the combined body heat of the spectators, attorneys and venire to warm the room to an acceptable level.

The jury pool comprised fifty people. Twelve asked the judge to be excused for reasons ranging from being single parents to running sole proprietorships to medical reasons; Yates excused nine.

The first twelve entered the jury box, and both sides questioned them. Only three said they were familiar with the case, and two admitted to having formed an opinion. The judge excused the pair and added two more. McAllister had told me that if he had his way, all twelve jurors would be female schoolteachers, but Allston's attorney dispatched the only teacher who entered the box.

We got rid of two men, the owner of an office supply store who did business with the county, a challenge which the court upheld, and a rancher prominent in political circles, whom we had to remove with one of our three peremptory challenges.

Back and forth we went—judge, plaintiff, and defense—until we'd settled on a dozen people and two alternates. Judge Yates told them to neither discuss the case with anyone nor watch or listen to media reports and dismissed them for the day.

We spent the last two hours arguing technical motions before the judge, winning two minor points, but losing all the important ones. "This will be a slog," Ben McAllister said over dinner.

———

On Wednesday morning, the two sides presented opening statements. Allston's attorney, Ralph Sommers, was a good old boy who appeared to be in his seventies; he had craggy, weather-worn features and a gray mane of hair that sprouted like dandelion seeds about to be scattered by the wind.

"We all know why we're here," he began, although the jurors had all sworn they knew nothing about the case and therefore shouldn't have had any idea. "My client, Brill Allston, is one of us, a local man who built a successful ranching business in the harsh conditions of high desert country and then turned to a life of public service."

Sommers turned from Allston to the jury, leaning against the wooden face of the jury box with both hands. "He spent a dozen years improving the lives of those in Franklin County, building roads, extending public utilities, and enhancing local law enforcement. Then, on the retirement of the incumbent state senator, he offered himself for that office, a position that pays less than chairman of the county commission—hardly the action of a venal man."

Two in the jury box nodded agreement. I wasn't certain either of them knew what venal meant, but Sommers had convinced them that Allston wasn't.

"And then," he said, turning toward our table, "a big city newspaper tried to deny you the right to his service. They printed a story accusing him of scandalous, self-aggrandizing behavior. If what they printed were true, I couldn't represent the man."

His voice lowered to a whisper. "But it wasn't. It isn't. We will show you that Senator Allston's opponent supplied the reporter with forged documents, and that the reporter quoted witnesses selectively and outright misquoted them. He even taped their conversations without permission, and that, my friends, is against the law."

Sommers crossed to our table and stood before me. "You will learn that this reporter, Mr. Alan Rudberg, who lives in one of Portland's most fashionable neighborhoods—"

Asa Miner rose to his feet and objected. The judge sustained the objection, but Sommers had made the point.

"Mr. Rudberg, editor of a big city newspaper, had a long-standing antipathy toward Senator Allston, holding him up to public ridicule when he tried to represent the interests of this county before state officials, and altering news stories to paint him in the worst possible light. This false and malicious reporting caused the senator to dig into his own pocket to counter the story." Sommers shook his head in mock distress.

Most of the jurors showed no reaction, but at least four scowled at me. We would have to work to counter the impression the old attorney had created.

McAllister made the attempt. "Howdy, everyone," he said. He'd doffed his suit coat, loosened his tie, and rolled up his sleeves. "My name is Ben McAllister. I too come from rural Oregon, born and raised in Redmond. I represent Mr. Alan Rudberg, the political editor of the *Oregon Examiner*, a man who bears no relationship to the description you've just heard."

McAllister took the jury through my career, how I paid my way through the University of Texas by working summers at a newspaper in Seguin, began my career with the *Examiner* reporting from Vancouver, Washington, and worked my way up to my present position, along the way collecting five AP awards, one of which was for a series on the effect of low property tax revenue on rural schools.

"The job of a reporter is to report," he said. "It's not to ignore unpleasant facts, promote one view or candidate over another, or try to sway people's minds. It's to research, investigate, and convey what he finds without fear or favor. Above all, it is to hold public officials accountable for their policies and actions. In this role, a reporter acts as your advocate. Not all of us can question the actions of public officials directly, so we depend on journalists like Mr. Rudberg to act as our surrogates. It is as much a life of public service as one spent chairing a county commission. *But without the opportunity to profit from it.*"

McAllister let his words linger before resuming. "As we will show, that's what Mr. Rudberg did. He received evidence suggesting that, as chairman of the county commission, Mr. Allston solicited and received payoffs from contractors who desired to work for the county. My client examined documents, talked with witnesses, and spent many hours traveling throughout Eastern Oregon to gather information. He then tried to present what he'd learned to Mr. Allston before printing a word of this, but Allston avoided and rebuffed him. In an abundance of fairness, Mr. Rudberg traveled from Portland to Pendleton for the sole purpose of interviewing

Allston—to give him a chance to correct the record and tell his side of the story."

Now McAllister moved before Allston's table. "Not only did Allston not take advantage of the opportunity afforded him, he threatened my client with a lawsuit if he even tried to tell the story— if he tried to do his job by telling you what he'd learned about what was happening to your tax dollars."

Returning to our side of the courtroom, he said, "Alan Rudberg is a responsible, respected journalist doing his job to protect your interests. He is not a partisan. He bears no ill will toward Mr. Allston. He never met the man until last October when he flew to Pendleton to interview him. He holds no malice toward Allston despite finding abundant evidence of his wrongdoing."

The attorneys had lunch brought in. We wanted no one in town kibitzing over our strategy sessions. I told McAllister I thought he had done well. "I didn't know you were from Redmond."

"Lived there until I was five," he said, without a trace of irony.

"And he was the only one of us who could stand before that jury," his more acerbic partner said. "'Hello, *leydiz aun jentalmin*, I'm Asa Miner, a Jewish boy from Queens.' It doesn't have the same ring to it." I honored his self-deprecation with a laugh.

"But what's this business about altering news stories about Allston?" said McAllister.

"I have no idea. After you brought that one story to my attention, I combed through the file trying to find any other references I've made to him. There were none."

"It sounds as though he's referring to stories written by others."

"My title is editor. That's what I do. I edit stories submitted by reporters on my team."

"Is it possible—?"

"Wait a minute." I told them about my contentious parting with Traci Jacobs three weeks before.

"Would she have written anything about Allston?"

"Sure. Even though she lived miles away, Franklin County was part of her beat." I explained how she covered the vast distances of Eastern Oregon. Traci would receive a news release or read a story in a local weekly, make calls to follow up on it, and submit her story for publication. As editor, it was my job to decide if it would run, and to make any needed changes to her copy before printing it.

"Has she turned on you?"

"It's possible." I told him it was Traci who had ferreted out the information on Ralph Weaver's death.

"So much for your fingerprints not being on that part of the investigation," Miner said.

I didn't argue with him. I couldn't see what difference it made. Weaver was dead, and the opposition knew he had been my original source.

———

Muriel Hendricks, the finance chair of Allston's senate campaign committee, took the stand after the lunch break. She was a slender, middle-aged woman with towering hair who overlooked the world through a pair of horn-rimmed bifocals perched at the bridge of a long, narrow nose, conveying the impression that she found everyone and everything a bit wanting. She testified that after my story ran, Allston put $18,000 of his own money into the campaign to pay for a letter to voters denying the charges.

What effect had my article had? "Oh, sir, it shocked us. It threw us into a tailspin. We all know Senator Allston and knew he'd do nothing like that, but the voters didn't, so we had to spend the money to set the record straight."

"And what else did it cost you besides money?"

"Time and effort. It set us back. We were hard at work on the campaign, and suddenly this."

On cross-examination, Asa Miner said, "Was this the first time Mr. Allston put money into his campaign?"

"Well, he'd loaned money in the past, but this was the first time he'd given it."

"And this mailing to voters, was it the first such communication he'd sent?"

She said it was, but Miner introduced copies of four letters mailed near the end of each of the prior months. "So it wasn't unusual for the campaign to send out a mailing, was it?"

"We'd done it before," she admitted, "but this is the first time we'd sent out a mailing like this, denying these charges."

Miner brandished a sheaf of campaign finance reports. "How much remains in the Allston for Senate campaign fund?"

She hemmed and hawed, saying she wasn't certain. "Does $78,000 sound about right?"

"Could be," she said.

"That's what your latest campaign report says."

"There may be outstanding bills."

"May be, but you're not sure. Still, the campaign will show a surplus, won't it?"

"Yes," she said in a voice that suggested this was of little consequence.

"So Mr. Allston can repay himself $18,000 whenever he wishes to, correct? But he's chosen not to, so he can claim that my client's story cost him money."

Mrs. Hendricks did not respond, while Sommers screamed his objection.

Hal Meredith followed. He no longer looked dapper, dressing in blue jeans, a plaid shirt, and the ubiquitous insulated vest. *Just one of the boys*, his outfit said.

After establishing his identity and role in the community, Sommers directed his attention to his successful paving bid. "Defendant Rudberg claimed—"

"Objection!" Asa Miner was on his feet. "Mr. Rudberg is not a defendant. He and his newspaper are respondents in a civil suit."

Judge Yates looked at him for several seconds before sustaining the objection, allowing the jury to sense his annoyance at the interruption.

"*Respondent* Rudberg," Sommers said, making the word sound worse than the original, "claimed in his story that the county awarded you the contract even though you were the high bidder. Is that correct?"

"No, sir. We bid on the paving job, but the county rejected all the responses and issued a new RFP. We were the sole bidder, got the contract, and did a quality job. These guys," he said, nodding at our table, "drove in on that road this morning. There's nothing wrong with it."

"Was this your first contract with the county?"

"No, sir. We've been serving Franklin County for over fifty years. My father started this company—" And Meredith launched into a long recitation of the firm's history and its work for the county.

"Defendant Rudberg also says you made an illegal payment to Senator Allston through the fictitious purchase of more than five thousand pounds of beef from his ranch. Is that true?"

"No, it's not." Miner let Sommers' use of the word *defendant* ride. To object would be to underline the slur in the minds of the jurors.

"He had an invoice that appears to show that," Sommers said.

"I know nothing about such an invoice. It's a hoax."

"Did you order any beef from Senator Allston's ranch?"

"Years ago, I may have. They're a local ranch. Everyone does business with them from time to time." Meredith looked at the jury, his glance suggesting that some of them might have done so.

"Did Senator Allston ever ask you for a bribe?"

"No, sir."

"Have you ever offered or given Senator Allston a payment of any sort to facilitate a contract?"

"No, sir. I wouldn't do that. That's not how I conduct business."

"Now, on the day Defendant Rudberg interviewed you, did you notice anything out of the ordinary?"

"You mean the tape recording?"

Sommers said as much, and Meredith recounted seeing me pocket my recorder at the end of the interview. "Did he ask in advance if he could tape the conversation?"

"No, he did not."

"And what was his reaction when you caught him—?" Miner lodged an objection, but the judge overruled him.

"He was sneaky about it," Meredith said. "He tried to put it away before I could stop him, but I demanded that he erase it."

"And did he?"

"He argued with me, said it was evidence in his case against Senator Allston, and he wouldn't give it up. But I made him."

"Did he say anything else to you about Senator Allston?"

"Yes, he said he would get him, regardless of whether I cooperated."

"'Get him.' He used those words?"

"Yes. 'I'm going to get him.' That's what he said."

Sommers thanked him, expressing his gratitude for his service to the county as though he were a philanthropist. Then it was McAllister's turn.

Holding the invoice before him, he said, "This is your signature, isn't it?"

"No, it doesn't look like mine at all."

"Your honor, I offer into evidence a handwriting analysis from the firm of Crocker and Company, stating that—"

"Objection," Sommers said. "This is not best evidence."

"The plaintiff has a point. Is your expert on hand to testify?"

"We can produce him, your honor."

"Then do so. Until then, restrict your questions to the evidence."

"You bid on a paving contract. The county received three proposals. Yours was highest. They made no award, rebidding the same project. You submitted the same proposal as you had previously, and yours was the sole bid. You got the contract and got the work. Is that true?"

"Yes, that's what I said."

"How do you explain that, the county rebidding the same contract and awarding it to the previous high bidder?"

"There were changes to the project."

McAllister presented three more contracts Meredith had won, all involving change orders made after they awarded the contract. "Isn't that how the county typically handles changes with you? They don't rebid the contract. They ask for the change and negotiate the price difference. Isn't that true?"

"That's sometimes the way it works."

"Why not in this case?"

"I don't know. You'll have to ask them."

"Now, Mr. Meredith, you made a $10,000 contribution to Mr. Allston's campaign for state senate."

"There's nothing illegal about that. Oregon has no limit on campaign contributions."

"Had you ever contributed such an amount to any previous campaign?"

"I'm not sure."

"I have the records here," McAllister said, picking up a file from our table. "That's a lot of money. It doesn't seem like something you'd forget."

McAllister asked three different ways, until Meredith admitted it was the most he'd ever given a candidate for any office. "Why did you make such a large contribution in this case?"

"Because I support Senator Allston," he said, his voice betraying an edge of sarcasm.

"And we're to believe there's no other reason. Four of your executives wrote checks for $2,500 each. Where did they get that kind of money?"

"I pay them well."

"Not that well." McAllister read off a list of names and salaries and asked if his information was correct. Meredith supposed so. "So $2,500 is a lot of money for them. Did you repay them?"

Meredith said he did not, and McAllister pressed him. "Are you aware it's illegal to make campaign contributions under a false name in Oregon? If you directed your employees to make gifts you later repaid, you committed a felony."

Meredith squirmed in his chair and cleared his throat. "2008 was a good year. I made generous year-end bonuses, but there was no connection."

"And 2008 was such a good year because you'd received a favorable contract from Mr. Allston, isn't that right?"

"Objection!" Sommers made a production of sounding exasperated. Judge Yates sustained the objection, but McAllister had made his point.

"Now about that tape recording. You claim that when you realized my client was taping the conversation, he tried to conceal it. But isn't it a fact that he apologized, that he—not you—offered to erase it, and that he did so in your presence?"

"No, I made him do it."

"You also claim he said he was out to get Mr. Allston. He never said that, did he?"

"No, he said it."

"You were not a willing source on this story, were you?"

"Willing? Of course not. I know Senator Allston and like him."

"Have you ever known or heard of a case of a reporter saying to any source—let alone an unfriendly one—that he was out to 'get' the subject of a story?"

"I wouldn't know. I don't know many reporters."

"What was your major at the University of Oregon?"

"Relevance!" Sommers shouted.

McAllister promised to show relevance, and the judge allowed Meredith to answer. "Journalism," he said.

McAllister smiled. "That's your degree, isn't it? BA in Journalism?"

"Yes."

"So when you say you don't know many reporters, that's untrue, isn't it?"

Meredith did not answer.

"Are you aware of the penalty for perjury?"

"Objection!"

"Withdrawn. Your honor, I ask permission to continue my cross-examination when our handwriting expert can appear."

I had dinner alone, poking at it, aware of what a fight lay ahead. Allston was all in on this case, willing to suborn perjury to restore his reputation and destroy mine. His contractor buddies seemed willing to help him do it.

I ventured out in the freezing weather for a walk—a small bit of exercise as recompense for hours of enforced sitting—and returned to my room for an early night's sleep. I called Stephanie to wish her good night and learned that my sister had been trying to reach me. I'd silenced my cell phone during the afternoon hearing and had forgotten to turn the ringer back on. Cheryl had called three times.

"She sounded hysterical," Stephanie said, "said you need to call her tonight."

It had happened, I decided. Mom had fallen and broken her hip or contracted a serious illness. Ready for the worst, I dialed Cheryl's number.

"I've been trying to reach you all day." I apologized, but she rushed forward without awaiting an explanation. "I'm moving her this weekend. She can't live on her own anymore."

"Have you talked to her about this?"

"I've told her this is the way it has to be, and that you and I are in agreement. I expect you to support me."

I gripped my cell phone, my hand shaking. "Cheryl, how could you do that without discussing it with me first?"

"Don't ask me that. I'm here with her. You're not. I'm responsible for her. The burden falls on my shoulders." *So this is all about you.* I didn't say it. "Are you coming to help, or are you going to sit gazing at the mountains, thinking great thoughts?"

"For the record, I am sitting in a motel room in a godforsaken corner of this state fighting a libel case that could cost my newspaper big money. It's impossible for me to get away."

"Fine. Think only of yourself. You're good at that."

I got off the phone, looked at the calendar, and called Asa Miner's room. "Monday is the Martin Luther King Jr. holiday, so we have a three-day weekend. I have a family emergency. I have to fly to Austin after court tomorrow. I'll be back Tuesday morning."

He agreed, making me promise to keep my cell phone handy in case he needed to talk.

The lead witness Friday morning was an older man who, on entering the box and removing his John Deere cap, revealed a bald pate surrounded by a fringe of dull brown hair. His nose was his most prominent feature, a network of crimson veins sprawling like roads on an urban map. He held his cap in one hand, kneading it, then passing it to the other hand. He identified himself as Mack Frawley. "Have you ever seen the defendant before?" Sommers asked.

"Yeah, I saw him in Pendleton on September 24."

"What was he doing?"

"Having lunch."

"Alone?"

"Yeah, until he got up to leave. Then another man joined him."

"This other man, did you know who he was?"

"Not at the time, but when I followed him to his car and saw the campaign sticker—you know those sheets of film they put on the sides of cars at NASCAR races? He had one of those plastered on the side of his Subaru. Then I saw his picture on a campaign billboard and knew who he was."

"Would you identify this other individual?"

"Nate Pearson, Senator Allston's opponent."

My heart sank. It was what I'd feared when Pearson approached me in front of the crowd of older men in early fall.

"What was their demeanor?"

"They were walking together, talking like they were sharing a secret."

Asa Miner objected, and the judge ordered the jury to ignore everything but our walking together.

"Did you overhear their conversation?"

"Sure. This guy Pearson, the schoolteacher, he said he knew Rudberg was working on a story that could harm Senator Allston and wanted to know when he would print it."

"Pearson said he knew about a story that had not been published, did he? And what did Rudberg say?"

"He kind of smiled—like they were in it together, you know?"

"Objection." The judge sustained it and ordered Frawley to stick to the facts.

"What did Defendant Rudberg say to Senator Allston's political opponent?"

"He asked him a bunch of questions about what he knew, what the senator had done. Rudberg told him the story would be published soon, and he'd let Pearson know."

"Did you get the impression they were in collusion with each other?"

"Objection."

"I'll let the witness answer this one."

"That they were in cahoots, you mean? Sure. They were talking quiet-like, but then this reporter, Rudberg, raised his voice so everyone in the lobby could hear and made this statement about how he was a reporter and he wasn't working for Pearson."

"And what did you take from that?"

"That my buddies and I had caught them meeting about some story and this reporter was putting on a show about how he wasn't working for the senator's opponent. He wanted us to hear it, you know?"

I whispered my version to Asa Miner, who thought about it for a second and rose to cross-examine the witness. "Mr. Frawley, did Mr. Rudberg approach Mr. Pearson, or was it the other way around?"

"I couldn't tell. Like I said, I was in the lobby with my buddies, waiting to be seated. They entered the lobby together."

"But earlier you testified he was having lunch alone. How could you know that if you were in the lobby?"

Frawley shifted in the witness chair. "I saw him from the lobby."

"But you didn't know who Mr. Rudberg was at the time, did you? Just a man sitting alone having lunch. How could you single him out?"

Frawley did not answer.

"Did you hear Mr. Rudberg ask how Pearson knew he was working on a story?"

"No."

"Did you hear Mr. Rudberg ask if Pearson had any concrete information?"

"No."

"So all you heard was what they discussed in the lobby, not the full exchange. You heard Mr. Rudberg trying to shake Pearson off, telling him he wasn't beholden to him."

"That's what he said, but he said it so we could hear it."

"That's your interpretation, isn't it? But that isn't what you heard."

Frawley shrugged.

Over lunch, the attorneys discussed adding Nate Pearson to the witness list. I apologized for failing to tell them about my chance meeting with him, but McAllister said, "I'm surprised you didn't reach out to him. I would have. If Pearson's solid, we can neutralize that testimony. I'm more concerned with this next witness. Take us through the story again."

Traci Jacobs didn't look at me as she entered the courtroom. She sat in the witness chair, took the oath, and stared at Sommers with what I took to be a look of smug self-satisfaction. Sommers had her identify herself and her profession, establishing that she had reported to me throughout her career.

"Was Mr. Rudberg a thoughtful boss?"

"Not particularly. When he wanted you to do something, he simply told you to do it. You'd ask him a question about working conditions, and he'd ignore it. I had to nag him about things that were important to me."

"Did you find him to be a fair man?"

"No. When I'd submit a story to him, he'd sometimes twist my words."

"Can you give us an example?"

"I wrote a story about Senator Allston—he was county commissioner then—requesting an increase in road funds from the state. When the *Examiner* printed the story, Rudberg had added a line." She opened a file and removed a clipping. "'For the past two budget years, Franklin County has received more state road funds on a per capita basis than any other county.'"

"So what did you take from that?"

"He didn't even ask me before putting it under my name. I thought he had it in for Senator Allston." Traci nodded her head as though to confirm her theory.

"Had anything else happened that led you to that conclusion?"

"Yes, I submitted a story in which I'd described Commissioner Allston as a 'leading political figure in Eastern Oregon.'" Traci read from a page of copy, putting air quotes around her words. She picked up a newspaper clipping. "But when my story ran, Rudberg had eliminated those words and substituted, 'chairman of the Franklin County Commission.'"

Sommers asked to admit both documents as evidence, then, turning to the jury, said, "So defendant Rudberg removed wording you used to describe the prominent role Senator Allston enjoys in this region and substituted words that made him sound like any other politician?"

Traci agreed with the interpretation.

"And when you learned that he was pursuing a story that would make Senator Allston look bad in the middle of his campaign, were you surprised?"

"Not at all. I knew he didn't like him."

"Objection."

"Overruled." Miner scrawled on his notepad, drawing a large ring around the entry.

"Did he use you to gather information on this story?"

"Yes, he did." Traci described how she'd accompanied me to my meeting with Allston in Pendleton. She told how I'd later asked her to locate Ralph Weaver.

"Did he give you any other instructions?"

"He said I wasn't to tell anyone in the clerk's office who I was or why I was calling."

"Is that unusual?"

"He'd never asked me to conceal my identity before."

"And why did he want you to do so on this occasion?"

"He didn't say, but I figured he was Rudberg's source for the forged documents."

"Objection," McAllister said. "The witness is stating a conclusion about the provenance of the documents."

"Sustained. The jury will ignore the witness's belief that the documents were forged." *Jesus! Nothing like upholding the objection by underlining it. Thanks, Judge.* Asa scrawled another note on his legal pad.

Sommers asked her to describe my reaction on learning of

Weaver's death. "Did the defendant accept the medical examiner's conclusion that Mr. Weaver died by his own hand?"

"No, definitely not. He said he didn't think Weaver would do that."

"What do you think he meant by that?"

"That he thought Senator—"

"Objection. Calls for a conclusion." But the damage had been done.

Asa Miner handled the cross-examination, the bad cop on display. "Why do you no longer work for the *Examiner*?"

"They fired me," Traci said, looking at me for the first time.

"And you blame Mr. Rudberg for that."

"He did it."

"Has he replaced you with anyone else?"

"Not to my knowledge."

"So is it possible that your termination resulted from staff reductions at the newspaper, rather than an action aimed specifically at you?"

"I wouldn't know."

"Were others terminated at the same time?"

"How would I know that?"

"Ms. Jacobs, who hired you at the *Examiner*?"

"He did. Mr. Rudberg."

"And what was your prior experience?"

She paused before speaking, gulped, and looked down at her hands. "He hired me after my graduation."

"So you had no prior experience, yet he took you on?" She didn't answer. "Did he make you bureau chief right away?"

"No, he had me report from Bend and The Dalles, then work with the bureau chief in Newport for a month."

"And then he promoted you?"

"Yes," she said, her voice growing quiet as she sensed where this was headed.

"Mr. Rudberg is the political editor at the paper, isn't he? Do you know what that job entails?" Traci listed several tasks, none of which involved editing stories. The attorney asked her whether copy editing was part of my duties, and she admitted to the possibility.

"Mr. Rudberg removed your reference to Mr. Allston being a political force in Eastern Oregon. Would you call that an editorial comment?"

"It's true."

"Who says that? Who's your source for that statement? Did you quote someone who used that characterization?"

"No."

"So it was your opinion, wasn't it? An editorial comment, not a substantiated fact? And your editor removed it. Is that the only occasion on which your editor excised an editorial statement from one of your stories?"

Miner picked up a file that I suspected contained nothing relevant to this line of questioning, but Traci fell for it. "No."

"He did so many times in many stories concerning many individuals, didn't he?" No answer.

"And the statement he added about Franklin County receiving more funds from the state highway trust fund than any other county on a population basis—isn't that a fact?"

"I don't know."

"Why not? You're a reporter, aren't you? This was your story."

She remained mute.

"The *Examiner* laid off over twenty percent of its editorial staff last month, closing two bureaus and reducing its capital bureau by one-half. They eliminated twenty positions in Portland alone. But you blamed your mentor, the man who hired you out of college, trained you, and kept you despite all your editorial errors. And you set out today to ruin him, didn't you? After all he's done for you."

Traci wept. She said nothing. I shook my head, willing him to stop.

"I have no further questions of this—uh—*witness*."

CHAPTER EIGHT
JANUARY 10-14, 2009

C ourt adjourned at four. I drove north to Pendleton, licking my wounds after the thrashing Traci had given me. I had hired her on her graduation from Eastern Oregon University, trained her, promoted her, supported her career, and now she had betrayed me. She was angry—I understood that—but she was inexperienced and had personalized a cold-hearted business decision.

Corporate America is impersonal and cares little for the lives of those who generate its profits, but Traci was myopic. She'd given no thought to the potential ramifications of her testimony. If we lost, the ruling would cascade across the entire profession, making journalists think twice before investigating wrongdoing of elected officials.

Even if we prevailed, Traci's career was over. By inventing her story and turning against me, she had ensured that no news organization would ever hire her. I took no satisfaction from it.

To get to Austin, I had to fly out of Pendleton to Portland, where Stephanie met me. We dined in one of the airport's excellent restaurants, during which I described Traci's testimony and how Miner had eviscerated her. "But you're still confident you'll win?"

"After today, yes, I am. We're bringing in expert testimony

Tuesday to prove their main witness is lying. I'm optimistic about the outcome."

She let out a long sigh. "Good, I'm relieved."

Shortly after nine o'clock, I boarded a flight to Austin, losing two hours across the time zones, and didn't turn in at an airport hotel until the middle of the night. The week-long court battle and the trip had worn me out; I was in no mood for jousting with Cheryl over Mother.

I arose at eight, grabbed a cup of coffee in the lobby, and headed to Mother's, where I hoped I could find something for breakfast. Cheryl had already arrived. The front porch held four packs of boxes of varying sizes. She stood there eyeing them as though they would open themselves. "About time you got here," she said.

I ignored her and went inside to find Mother, who sat on her sofa blubbering. "I can't believe my children would do this to me."

"Mom, it's in your best interest. This house needs a lot of work; there's no one here to tend to it. If you were to fall, no one is nearby to help you. The neighborhood is changing—you've said so yourself— and you'll meet friends at your new home who share your interests."

What she'd really said was that "Meskins" were "taking over" the neighborhood, but this was mild compared to what she'd had to say about the president-elect.

Cheryl had cleaned out the kitchen, so I drove a few blocks for a box of donuts—which I would never have eaten under ordinary circumstances—and a container of coffee. We spent the day winnowing Mother's things, packing what she was taking, and taping and marking boxes. I asked her about one unopened container. "It's a replacement mask for my CPAP."

"Is this what I ordered for you? Why aren't you using it?"

"I'm using the one you bought, Sonny. Once I had the machine operating, the company called and said, since I was using it again, I qualified for a replacement mask." This made as much sense as anything else she told me that weekend.

Mother quarreled over items that no longer had utility in the small kitchen to which she was moving and kept foisting "keepsakes" on us that had neither real nor sentimental value. I placed mine in a box, took it back to my hotel that night, and left it behind when I returned to Oregon.

On Sunday morning, two Hispanic men arrived with a rented truck, loaded her furniture and boxes aboard, and drove them to her new home. After we arrived at the building, Mother went downstairs to the dining room while Cheryl and I unpacked. When Mother returned, she went into her bedroom in tears. Something had happened, but she wouldn't say what.

While she laid down for an afternoon nap, Cheryl sat with me at the small dining table to finalize the financial arrangements. She was selling Mother's house to make the required deposit on her apartment. The rest, along with her social security check, would cover the monthly rent, at least until it increased. Cheryl and I would pitch in to provide living expenses.

"I never wanted my children to do for me." Mom had been eavesdropping at her bedroom door. She'd heard every word. I knew what was coming next.

"If I hadn't been on my own, I could have saved something. But your father left us, walking away without a care in the world. He didn't contribute a dime to your welfare—"

"I know, Mom," I said.

"I did it all myself. I raised you kids with no help from that man, and this is what it's come to. You're having to do what he should have done."

"Don't worry about all this. We can handle it. You've done for us all your life. Now it's our turn," Cheryl said.

We had dinner in the facility's dining room. Choices were chicken breast, beef stew, and a fish called swai that I'd never heard of and, having had it that evening at Mother's table, never hope to again. Cheryl settled for the chicken and Mother for the beef stew. "I hate the food here," she said. "I had chicken salad for lunch. They had *watercressnuts* in it. I hate *watercressnuts*."

I told her I hated them, too. Once we were served, she revealed what had upset her at lunch. When she'd taken an empty chair at a table, the other women had told her that all the seats were reserved. She'd sat on her own at an empty table until another newcomer took refuge with her. "And she was so old."

She wept. I looked around, feeling conspicuous and embarrassed, but no one paid any attention to us. Either they were used to these reactions among newcomers or didn't care. "I am so *flustrated,*" she said as she blubbered. I didn't bother to correct her. Flustrated seemed like the right word.

I felt guilty but helpless. This is not what she'd bargained for in life. I resented how Cheryl had made me the bad guy, but I had offered no alternative, save a move to Portland, which neither of them would countenance.

At that moment, I resented my father, a man whom I only vaguely remembered. Like me, he was a journalist, though I did not admire his work. I had resolved to be nothing like him, and I'd succeeded, building a happy family, never straying from my devotion to Stephanie and Eric.

I also resented the constant reminders of his faults from my mother and sister. From my earliest memory, every interaction with Mother devolved into a denunciation of my father and a recitation of his failings. No son needs to hear this about his father. The only way to avoid her lectures was to avoid her, so that's what I'd done throughout my adult life.

I boarded an evening flight to Portland, regaining the two hours I'd lost on the way down, slept in my bed for the first time in more than a week, and was back at the airport at noon for the journey back to Center City, almost welcoming the diversion after the weekend with my mother and sister.

Jim Jeffreys, the clerk of circuit court, took the stand Tuesday morning. He testified about my visit to the courthouse that hot day in

August that now seemed so long ago, describing my request to see the file on a paving contract and my surprise when I found just a sole bid. "He was looking for something. He acted suspicious," Jeffreys said.

"Did he question you about it?"

"Yes, he wanted to know why there was only one bid. I explained we'd received just a single response to the RFP. He started cross-examining me why. I told him to ask other contractors, that I didn't know. He was rude."

"He expected something else to be there, is that correct? What did you take from that?"

"That someone had told him something he otherwise wouldn't have known."

"Following defendant Rudberg's visit, did you take any action?"

"I thought about where he got the idea there was something wrong with relisting the project."

"What did you decide?"

"One of my employees had acted suspiciously during Rudberg's visit. He followed everything we said. After Rudberg left, he asked what he'd learned. He nosed around, looking in files of projects that had gone before. He even hung around after hours, which wasn't like him."

"Who was this employee?"

"Ralph Weaver, my assistant clerk."

"What action did you take as his supervisor?"

"I sat him down—this was weeks later, in October, I think—and said, 'What are you up to?' Weaver denied he was helping this reporter, but I knew he was a Pearson man—"

"Nate Pearson, Senator Allston's opponent? What do you mean 'a Pearson man?'"

"I knew from campaign records that he'd contributed to him. I told him we have to be impartial, that I can't have someone in my office working to support one candidate or the other."

"How did Weaver react?"

"At first he denied talking with Rudberg, but he eventually

broke down and admitted it. When I say broke down, I mean he was snuffling and crying. Said he needed this job to support his mother. He was groveling. It disgusted me. Then I found out he'd been rifling through the chairman's office after hours, stealing documents. I didn't realize he was altering them, but stealing was bad enough."

Miner objected as stating a fact not in evidence, but Judge Yates overruled him. The reversible error was piling up.

"So what did you do?" Sommers asked.

"I told him I was terminating him, that he could either resign or I'd turn him over to the sheriff's office for breaking and entering."

"What did he do then?"

Jeffreys looked around the courtroom before answering. "I hate to say this, but he took his own life. I didn't mean for that to happen, and I'm sorry, but I can't have someone working in this office who takes advantage of his position for political purposes." He looked to the jury as though seeking their endorsement of his rectitude.

McAllister took on the cross-examination. "You had this confrontation with Ralph Weaver in October. When in October?"

"I don't recall."

"But you know when you took him off the payroll."

"Middle of the month."

"What led you to the conclusion that Mr. Weaver had accessed some of Mr. Allston's private records?"

"Because of things the reporter asked."

"And how did you know that?"

Jeffreys paused. "Everybody knew it."

"I'm not interested in what others knew. I'm asking about you. Who told you Weaver had handed the beef invoice to Mr. Rudberg?"

"I don't remember."

"It was Mr. Allston, wasn't it? Rudberg confronted him during the second week in October and asked him about several under-the-table transactions—"

"Objection."

"Withdrawn. Didn't Allston tell you Mr. Rudberg had asked about the beef invoice? Isn't that when you confronted Weaver?"

"He may have mentioned it. I don't recall."

"You don't recall. Perhaps you'll remember how you knew that Ralph Weaver had made a $50 contribution to Pearson's campaign."

"It's a public record."

"And so it is, but why would you look through campaign reports of Mr. Allston's opponent?"

"I'm the clerk of circuit court. All this paperwork goes through me."

"Don't campaign finance reports go through the secretary of state in Salem?" Jeffreys considered it for a moment, then acknowledged it. "Why would a man so obsessed with the neutrality of his office look at a piddling little contribution made to Commissioner Allston's opponent?"

Jeffreys shifted his considerable weight in the chair, slicked his hair back with both hands, but said nothing.

"I have no further questions for this witness."

The morning concluded with a parade of contractors who testified to Allston's good character and said he had never asked for a payoff of any sort—either as a campaign contribution or as a gift. McAllister posed enough questions to establish that all of them had given to the campaign, but, as one said, "There's no law against that."

We wondered whether Allston would testify. He had no obligation to do so, but while the senator was a popular figure in Franklin County and could boast about his many accomplishments, he would open himself to cross-examination if he took the stand. Both McAllister and Miner doubted he would do so, and when Sommers rested, they were proven correct.

Following the lunch break, McAllister called our handwriting expert to the stand. Michael Crocker was a Seattle-based expert witness who had testified in cases throughout the Northwest and British Columbia. He established the limitations imposed by the document he'd examined—a photocopy rather than the original—but stated that, in his expert opinion, the signature on the invoice for beef from Allston's ranch was identical to samples he'd obtained of Hal Meredith from public records.

"Since this is a photocopy, couldn't someone have pasted the signature from another document into this one?" McAllister asked.

Crocker called that unlikely. He brought up an image of the document on a large high-definition monitor we'd brought into the room. "I've increased the contrast here. You can see black dots showing imperfections in the paper. If someone had pasted in the signature, I would expect to see an outline around the signature itself, showing the area that had been clipped from another document. As you can see, there's a smooth gradation between the signature and the surrounding area, and the black dots continue up to the signature and within the loops."

He brought up a second image, focusing on detail at the bottom. "The signature was written over a straight printed line. Note the four areas, one in the capital 'F' and three in the capital 'M' where the ink drops below the line. If someone had pasted the signature in, he would have had to paint that line to match the original. The line is perfectly straight, with no deviation in width or depth."

"So from this you conclude...?"

"Although this is a photocopy, it's clear that the signature was written on the original document; it matches the other samples of Mr. Meredith's handwriting."

Attorney Sommers tried to shake Crocker's assertions about his ability to analyze a photocopy, but Crocker was an experienced hand and deflected the effort. He sought to undermine Crocker's insistence that the signature was Meredith's rather than a forgery, but when Crocker referred to visuals of the loops and swirls in the handwriting samples, Sommers changed the subject.

He brought up two court cases in which the defense had challenged Crocker's analyses. He conceded that no analysis is 100 percent accurate, that it depends on such variables as the quality of originals or copies, the expert's experience, and the quality of forensic tools. "The cases you cited occurred two decades ago. Since then, we've gained access to more sophisticated—"

"So no analysis is totally accurate. Thank you. One more question: You're not here as a volunteer, are you?"

"I'm a professional, if that's what you mean."

"You're paid. A hired gun."

"I'm paid for my expertise, as I assume you—"

"Move to strike," Sommers said.

"Sustained. The witness will answer only what he is asked."

But Crocker had acquitted himself well. With his testimony behind us, Asa Miner recalled Hal Meredith to the stand. The paving contractor denied that the signature was his.

"Do you understand," Miner said, "that if your company paid for something it did not receive, and if it listed the payment as a business expense on its tax return—"

"Objection."

"I haven't finished my question."

"Your honor," Sommers said, "he's intimidating the witness."

"Sustained."

"We haven't filed our 2008 return," Meredith said.

"Mr. Meredith..." Miner stared at him for a moment, giving him time to fidget. "Did you or did you not pay $24,500 to Allston for an order of beef you haven't received, and was that money not a payoff to Mr. Allston in return for approving your *high bid contract*?"

"No, it wasn't." Meredith looked to Allston for help. "It hasn't been delivered."

"What hasn't?"

"The beef. It's coming this spring. I paid in advance. It's—have you ever heard of futures? It happens all the time in agriculture. You pay a farmer or rancher for something he hasn't grown yet, locking in an attractive price."

From somewhere behind us, a few people chuckled, one snorting to suppress his laughter. Was he laughing at the transparency of Meredith's lie or the deftness with which he'd neutered the suggestion that there was a quid pro quo? Perhaps both.

"So when you testified under oath that the signature was not yours—"

"I knew you city folks wouldn't understand about futures. I tried to keep it simple."

"But it's not us 'city folks' you need to convince, is it?" Miner said, looking at the jury.

During the ensuing break, I said to Miner, "He committed perjury just now."

"So?" the attorney replied. Seeing the look of confusion on my face, he added, "Do you think the district attorney here is going to charge him? Do you think a local jury would convict him?"

Nate Pearson took the stand at mid-afternoon. Although in his early forties, he had a boyish look about him with clear, unlined features, a perpetual grin, and an uneven mop of blond hair that lay in only a general direction, as though he'd used his hands instead of a brush and comb. John Denver reincarnated, only better fed.

He answered Miner's introductory questions without shedding his smile, as though he considered it all a lark.

"Do you know my client, Alan Rudberg?" the attorney asked.

"No, but I spotted him in a restaurant in Pendleton back in September and had a brief conversation with him."

"Had you met him before that?" Pearson said he had not. "Have you seen or spoken with him since your first meeting?"

"Not until today."

Miner led him through our encounter, an accurate portrayal of everything that had transpired both within the restaurant and in the lobby. "Did he provide you with any information?"

"No, he was tight-lipped, told me I could read the story when he published it."

"Did he give you any details about his investigation?"

"No, I offered to help him, said everything he'd heard was true, but he didn't take me up on it. I was put off, to tell the truth."

"You asked him about a story he was working on concerning your opponent. How did you know about it?"

"A contractor told me he'd been asking questions." Under questioning, he identified his source as Silvio Bernardo, who'd called him shortly after I left his office. "It was common knowledge. Everyone knew a reporter from the *Examiner* was asking questions about Allston, but until Mr. Bernardo called me, I didn't know what it was all about."

"Do you know Ralph Weaver?"

"I never met him. I know he's dead now. They claim he committed suicide, but who knows?"

Allston's attorney could have objected but didn't. I assumed he didn't want to call attention to the inference.

"You never met with him concerning your campaign?" Miner asked the same question four different ways, getting uniform denials. Pearson had never contacted Weaver, Weaver had never contacted Pearson, Weaver had never sent Pearson any information about Allston, and Pearson was unaware that Weaver had contributed to his campaign.

On cross, Sommers said, "We all understand that you have to live here now that the campaign is over, so it wouldn't be to your advantage to admit that you conspired with a public servant to concoct false information about your opponent, would it?"

"Well, I didn't," he said. "Besides, I can say what I want. I'm moving to White Salmon, Washington in the spring."

Someone had made life uncomfortable for this boyish school teacher who had done battle with the area's state senator. They'd driven him out.

Silvio Bernardo, the Baker City contractor, finished the day. In response to McAllister's question, he described his business as "digging holes to hold water. We maintain reservoirs and dams, both public and private, construct tanks and cisterns—"

"And swimming pools?" McAllister prompted.

"Yes, we build and maintain swimming pools for towns, hotels, even homeowners," he said. The way he stated it suggested that residential pools were a rarity in this part of the state.

McAllister stepped him through his meeting with Allston. "You were the low bidder on the Mascall Reservoir project."

"That's right." Bernardo outlined the bidding process, the amount of his offer, and the experience he brought to the project. He described how Allston had visited him in his office and hinted that he wanted a pool built, how he'd outlined one pool while Allston negotiated for something larger. "I agreed to do the job and started work the following week."

"Was it usual for the chairman of a county commission to drive a hundred miles to discuss a pending contract with you?"

"Forget the drive. Not even our own commissioners do that."

"How much time elapsed between the date you learned you were the low bidder until Mr. Allston paid you a visit?"

"About a month."

"And during that time, you got no contract from the county?"

"I didn't hear a word."

"How long was it between the start of work on Mr. Allston's swimming pool and when you finally received a contract?"

"We got the go-ahead as soon as we started digging. They sent out the contract the next day."

McAllister turned him over to Sommers. "Isn't it the case that Senator Allston never asked you to build him a pool?"

"I told you, he hinted all around about it like a dog sniffing another one's butt." Laughter rocked the courtroom while the judge, suppressing a smile, banged his gavel.

"He never asked you to do anything. He found out you build pools and expressed interest, as any other person might. You gave him one, in effect trying to buy your way into a contract. But you needn't have done that because you were the low bidder."

Bernardo favored him with an amused smile. "Mister, I don't know what you do, but I don't go around digging holes for nothing." Laughter again filled the courtroom as Sommers moved to strike.

The contractor who had described leaving the $2,000 on Allston's desk testified next. Sommers also took him apart, establishing that he never saw Allston reach for the money and that he couldn't say it wasn't a campaign contribution. Allston hadn't included the money on his original campaign report, but he'd filed an amended report two weeks before the trial.

An equipment salesman, Ray Spurgis, took the stand. In September, he'd described Allston soliciting a $5,000 bribe in exchange for a contract to purchase a new backhoe. He'd been reluctant to speak to me in September, but Weaver had provided enough information to allow me to pry the truth from his clenched teeth. On the stand, however, he backtracked. "I didn't pay nothing to Senator Allston. The deal was all above board."

"Didn't you tell Mr. Rudberg that you had to pay Allston $5,000 before he would okay the contract?" Miner said.

"I never told him no such thing."

Turning to the judge, "Your Honor, I wish to introduce a recording of the conversation between—"

"Objection!" Sommers said. "Any recording of a conversation between Rudberg and this witness was made without his knowledge and is therefore inadmissible."

"Not so, Your Honor. The recording clearly shows—"

The judge called all three attorneys into his chambers. I remained at the defense table while Spurgis sat in the witness box. Neither of us looked at the other. Spectators milled about, talking among themselves while the minutes ticked by. It took more than a quarter hour before the group returned to the courtroom, Sommers grinning while McAllister and Miner scowled.

"I have no further questions for this witness," Miner said.

"What the hell—?" McAllister placed a firm hand on my arm.

Judge Yates called a recess until the following morning. Only then did I learn what had happened. "Sommers argued that because you didn't notify Hal Meredith you were taping him, none of the tapes are admissible."

"But the first words you hear on this tape are me informing Spurgis I was recording him," I said.

"True, but since the judge has ruled the tape inadmissible, the jury won't hear that—or anything else he said."

"The tape that proves Spurgis is lying can't be introduced because he says he wasn't aware he was being recorded, even though the tape shows he was. Is that about it?"

McAllister agreed. "The only bright spot is that it's as clear a case of reversible error as I've encountered." But his grim face suggested that was small recompense.

Over dinner, we discussed our remaining witnesses and removed two who we suspected would take advantage of the adverse decision on the admissibility of my recordings to alter their stories. We couldn't risk letting the jury hear their denials.

A day that had seemed so promising had turned menacing.

Silvio Bernardo was brave to testify against Allston, but he had had little at stake, as he didn't depend on Franklin County for business and was in a different senatorial district. Walter Grayson was another matter, since his business was in the adjoining county and thus the same district. I feared that, with so much to lose, he would fold when he took the stand.

I needn't have worried. From the moment he took the oath, he made clear he was an angry, righteous man.

"How did you get him to testify?" I'd asked McAllister at break-fast. "He was nervous when we met and refused to let me quote him."

"He called us," the attorney replied. "Once he learned about the lawsuit, he decided to get on the side of the angels."

I smiled at Grayson as he took his seat. He coughed into a hand-kerchief and waved. Asa Miner established his business, had him describe the history of his company and the number of government jobs he'd completed, and asked for details on the county road he'd repaved in Walker County.

"So when Franklin County put out its RFP for Mascall Road, why did you bid on it?"

"It's the same road, it was the same requirement. We'd done a good job for Walker County, and I knew they'd vouch for us. I knew what I could do it for and still make a profit, so I bid."

Miner asked him for the amount of his bid and what happened after he submitted it. "I attended the bid opening. I always do. Ours was the low bid. I figured I'd get a contract the next week, but nothing came. Then I got a notice saying they'd rejected all three bids because the project had changed. They were re-advertising it."

"Did you participate?"

Grayson laughed until he coughed—coughed so hard I feared he'd break a rib. After he recovered, he said, "No, I got the picture. They wanted it to go to someone else. It takes time to put bid docu-ments together—time you take away from your other projects. I don't have time to waste—didn't then and sure as hell don't now. I spoke with the third bidder, the one who'd come in between me and Mered-ith. We agreed it was pointless, so neither of us responded. Meredith submitted almost the same bid and walked away with it. I went and looked. The price was the same, just a few jiggers here and there to reflect the new timeline and all. He got the work, and Oregon's taxpayers got screwed."

Sommers objected. The judge agreed and instructed the jury to ignore Grayson's last comment. Miner wouldn't let it go. "If the county had accepted your bid and altered the scope through a change order—"

"The changes were minor. I wouldn't have charged them anything."

"How much would the county have saved?"

"Over six hundred thousand dollars."

"A lot of money," Miner said.

"Out here? Yes, sir, it's a great deal of money."

Sommers took over on cross-examination. "I want to be clear about a few things. Franklin County rebid the project, but you failed to respond. Only one company entered a bid, and they won the competition. You blame them. Is that your testimony? Yes or no?"

"It was hopeless."

"Yes or no?"

"Yes, but—"

"Thank you. Oh," he said, "you had to redo part of the project on the Walker County side, didn't you? You didn't do it right the first time."

"There was a problem with the grade at Marker 9.8 that wasn't apparent at the time. We fixed it."

"Thank you."

"But we didn't charge Walker County a penny."

"Objection. Move to strike," Sommers said.

"Sustained."

Miner wasn't having it. "I have two questions on redirect. Mr. Grayson, how much did you charge Walker County to repair the work at Marker 9.8?"

Grayson coughed into his handkerchief and peered at the jury. "Nothing. It wasn't even our mistake. The county engineer had missed it when he issued the RFP. It was supposed to be a straight repaving job, but there was a washout beneath the roadbed they hadn't caught. When the road began to sink, we filled in the hole and repaved it from the bed up. We didn't charge them a nickel."

"One more thing. When Mr. Rudberg interviewed you back in August, did you want to speak with him?"

"No, I told him not to quote me."

"And did he?"

"No. He said he wouldn't; he did as he promised."

"Why were you reluctant back then?"

"I'm a small businessman. I have to do business here. I can't afford to make enemies."

"But now you're here in court of your own volition. Why?"

Grayson looked at Asa Miner, flashed me a smile, turned to the jury, and said, "Two reasons. One, I want to do my part to stop this sort of thing. An honest man ought to be able to do honest work without having to pay someone off."

"And the other reason?"

Grayson coughed into his handkerchief and reached into his pocket, extracted a pack of cigarettes and held it up. "These got me. Where I'm headed, no one can touch me—only the good Lord."

Two women in the jury box gasped, as did I. It was the first favorable reaction I'd seen from them since the trial started, but at what a cost.

CHAPTER NINE
JANUARY 15-17, 2009

I took the stand Thursday morning. The Doons Bradberry pair had been prepping me for weeks and had spent two hours the previous evening leading me through what they would ask and the line they expected Sommers to take.

Miner conducted the direct examination. We thought my being questioned by the resident bulldog would impress the jury. In response to his questions, I presented my "B-copy"—my educational background, history at the *Examiner*, career highlights and awards, and a detailed description of what my job entailed.

He had me describe how the case had come to my attention—the anonymous envelope that had arrived at my desk the previous August. "Is it unusual to receive such a communication?"

"No. It doesn't happen every day, but several times a year I'll receive a call or a letter alerting me to something the paper should look into."

"And what do you do when you receive such information?"

"First, I have to decide whether it's worth pursuing. We don't have the resources to investigate every lead that comes our way. If it appears a story has merit, we have to delve into it."

"Why don't you just print it?"

"We can't do that. We're obligated to determine whether what we have—allegations, tips, documents, whatever—is true. When material comes anonymously, we try to find out who gave it to us. Is the source reliable? Does he or she have an axe to grind? We need to be sure we're not being used."

I described how I'd proceeded, taking them through my return trips to Eastern Oregon and my interviews with contractors.

"At some point, did you identify who sent you the material?"

I confirmed it and described the process of elimination I'd gone through.

"Even though you knew the identity of this source, you didn't identify him in your eventual story. Why was that?"

"He asked for confidentiality, and I agreed, after discussing it with my managing editor."

"Why did you agree? Wouldn't it have been preferable to name him?"

"I prefer to identify anyone who contributes information to a story, but it's not always possible. Some sources can't risk being involved. Witnesses to violent crimes often fear the perpetrators will come after them. Someone working for a company fears he'll be fired. I could name five or six other instances in which I've needed to protect a source. Working with my editor, I evaluate each one. It's legal. Oregon has a shield law that allows reporters to protect sources of information."

"Why did you conceal the identity of this source?"

"He feared his employer would retaliate. He was right."

"You've refused to name him in the past. Would you do so now?"

I turned to the jury. "There are many cases in which reporters have refused to name sources, even if they risk prison sentences. Many will protect a source even after he's passed away; I did that in one case. But here, Mr. Jeffreys has already revealed his identity. He was the assistant clerk, Ralph Weaver."

"Did you ask how he got these documents?"

"Yes, but he wouldn't answer. I had to verify them through interviews. We had a lot going on last fall with the senate and presidential elections, but I visited Eastern Oregon four times to pin down the story."

"Did you try to interview Mr. Allston?"

"Numerous times. I called his office and his home; I left messages with everyone I reached. He never responded. When I learned he was speaking in Pendleton, I flew there to intercept him. It cost time and money, but I wanted to get his side of the story."

"And did he agree to speak with you?"

"He did not. He told me to speak to his staff, which I'd already done. I asked him about soliciting the swimming pool from Mr. Bernardo in exchange for the contract. He denied it. I asked about the $24,500 contract for beef from his ranch as a quid pro quo. He denied having anything to do with county contracts. I included those denials in my story."

I again turned to the jury. "He was racing for his car and told me that if I printed this story, he would sue me. And so he has."

"If he had sat down and talked with you—?"

"He might have been able to clarify the allegations made against him. Or perhaps not. In either case, I would have reported everything he said—denials, excuses, counter-allegations, whatever."

"Mr. Rudberg, had you ever met Mr. Allston before you began working on this story?"

"I saw him at a meeting of county commissioners in Portland two years ago, but I didn't meet him."

"Have you ever told anyone you were 'out to get' Mr. Allston?"

"No, I would never do that."

"Have you ever edited another reporter's story to make Mr. Allston look bad?"

"No. The edits that Ms. Jacobs referred to were, in one case, to remove her characterization of Mr. Allston that represented an editorial comment and, in the other, to report a pertinent fact she had failed to research. That's my job. It's what editors do."

"And when she says she knew you didn't care for Mr. Allston—?"

"At no time did I discuss Mr. Allston with her before I began working on the story, while I researched it, or after the *Examiner* published it. I can't say why she believes that, but it's not based on anything I said or did. I'm a journalist, not an advocate."

Miner had no further questions, but Allston's attorney, Jake Sommers, did. He paced before me, his hands knitted behind his back, his chest thrust out, eyeing me like a strange animal. "Mr. Rudberg," he said, but he asked no question for a moment. "Mr. Rudberg, you've been in journalism how long?"

"Twenty-five years."

"All with the *Oregon Examiner*?"

I told him about summers during my college years when I'd subbed for vacationing reporters on a small newspaper in the Texas Hill Country, a fact Miner and McAllister had already established.

"And Mr. Miner—" here he turned and stared at Asa as though he were a companion to this strange animal "—Mr. Miner says you've won awards over the years. Tell us about them."

"Five AP Awards," I said, naming the three stories and two columns that had produced them.

"You're proud of those, aren't you?"

Where was this leading? "I don't normally mention them, but they're given by my peers, so I suspect Mr. Miner wanted to establish that I have a good reputation within my profession."

"By your *peers!*" He spoke it as a sneer. "Very nice for you. And are these national awards?" I replied that they were regional.

"So during that time, you've never won a national award, have you?" Not waiting for an answer, he said, "Never another award, like —what's the big one? The name escapes me."

I doubted that, but answered, "The Pulitzer."

"The *Pew*-litzer," he said, mispronouncing it as he drew it out.

"That's the big one. Have you ever been nominated for the *Pew-litzer?*"

"Yes, once, and I was a finalist."

"But you didn't win it. That must be a source of great disappointment to you."

"Objection, you honor. Relevance."

"Mr. Miner," Judge Yates said, "you opened this line by citing Mr. Rudberg's previous awards. The plaintiff may question what other honors he's sought or received."

Miner gave up, giving me a slight shrug. If he didn't know what point Sommers was trying to make, I now did. He repeated the question.

"Not particularly," I said. "I'm not out for honors. They're nice, but they're not what motivates me, or most reporters I know."

"You don't care about awards, at least not about those you haven't received."

"Objection," McAllister said.

"You're the political editor of Oregon's largest newspaper. What does that job entail?"

"As I told Mr. Miner, I'm in charge of all reporters and bureaus covering politics and government for the *Examiner*. I edit much of the copy with the help of my assistant editor. I make assignments and decide which stories to run in the space allotted to us. I write a twice-weekly column, and I get to do some original reporting."

"Sounds like a lot of responsibility," he said. "How do you find time for all that?"

I didn't answer, since none seemed to be required.

"Besides this questionable story on Senator Allston, what else did you cover this fall?"

"I covered both Senate candidates and both Presidential campaigns."

"And both political conventions?"

I nodded in agreement, sensing where he was headed with this new line.

"When you say you covered both Presidential campaigns, what did that entail?"

"I spent a week each with Senators McCain and Obama."

He turned his back on me and leaned against the jury box. "So in the ten weeks between the time you received this anonymous package from Mr. Weaver until you ran the story, you spent four weeks out of state."

"And six weeks in the state," I countered.

"Covering the two candidates for the US Senate and doing all the other things you listed as a part of your important job." He paced for effect. "And investigating these allegations against Senator Allston, which required considerable travel to and from Portland."

"I first looked into this matter while covering Senator Smith in Pendleton," I said.

"So this investigation was a sideline—something you tacked onto visits here for other purposes."

There was no way to escape the narrative he had built. "I worked most weekends. I—"

"And you didn't come out here to spend a week or two talking to people, did you? You were back and forth, a day here, then off to see Obama. A day there, then travel with Senator McCain."

"I did considerable research from my office in Portland."

"Researching Franklin County from an office in Portland. That must have been useful. I'm curious what interest the political editor of the *Oregon Examiner* might have in a small county in rural Eastern Oregon."

"We cover news throughout the state and in southwest Washington, too."

"But to send the political editor of the state's largest newspaper to cover a story three hundred miles from Portland, that's unusual, wouldn't you say?"

"We're a statewide newspaper. I've covered stories from Ontario to Gold Beach," I said, citing communities at opposite ends of the state.

"While you were an editor, or while you were still a reporter?"

"I was a reporter for much of it."

"And during a year when you were covering two presidential and two statewide senatorial campaigns?"

I allowed him the point, matching his eye contact and waiting for his next thrust.

"Why do it yourself? Why not send one of your reporters, someone who knows Eastern Oregon, someone like Ms. Jacobs, for example?"

"She hadn't handled a story like this before. She didn't have the experience to take on an investigation of this scope."

"And you weren't about to give her that experience, were you? Perhaps you feared she wouldn't give it the right slant."

"There was no 'slant.' I received information that was suggestive. I needed to determine if there was enough basis to it to merit further investigation."

"When you first opened this *investigation*, who else knew about it?" I wasn't certain what he meant and said so. "That day in August when you drove from Pendleton to Central City to the clerk's office, who else knew you were coming here?"

"No one. I had received a packet of documents. I was in Pendleton covering Senator Smith. It was easy enough to make a side trip to Franklin County to look into it."

"You took an extra day away from the office, didn't you? Did you request permission from your managing editor?"

"No. I wouldn't ordinarily do so."

He turned to the jury. "Oh, you get to do what you want, is that what you're telling us?"

"Objection," Asa Miner shouted. "Your honor, this has no relevance to Mr. Allston's lawsuit. It has no bearing on whether the facts presented in this story are accurate."

"It goes to the defendant's motivation in traveling three hundred miles and taking a day and a half out of a busy schedule to make a case against my client, your honor."

"Sustained."

Sommers repeated the question. "I have considerable latitude in self-assigning, as long as I produce stories."

"So long as you produce stories. So if you had traveled all that way, taken all that time, and produced nothing, your editor might have asked questions?"

"No."

"No?"

"Not unless I made it a habit." I struggled to conceal my annoyance. Keep your cool, the attorneys had cautioned.

"You call the *Examiner* a statewide newspaper, but that's no longer the case, is it?"

"We are a newspaper that reports on our state and region, not only the Portland metropolitan area."

"A few weeks ago, right before Christmas, didn't you close two bureaus and cut your state bureau by half?"

"The publisher did, yes."

"And you've reduced your circulation area, I believe. Do you still have home delivery here in Franklin County?"

"No, but we did then."

"In Pendleton?"

"No. Financial conditions have forced the owners to reduce our service area, but that was—"

"But these 'financial conditions'—they didn't crop up a week before Christmas, did they?"

"I'm on the editorial side. I don't know how long this has been building."

"Still, wouldn't you agree it's strange for a newspaper that was about to cut bureaus and reduce its circulation area to allow one of its senior editors to go gallivanting around—"

"Objection."

"Sustained."

"Strange that a newspaper about to eliminate Franklin County from its service area would allow its political editor to make four trips and take several days out from a busy election year to go poking around in a rural campaign for state senate."

I didn't answer; it wasn't a question, and I knew Sommers was about to draw his own conclusion.

"But they didn't have the chance to stop you, because you didn't ask, did you?"

"Not at first, but after the initial visit, my editor was well aware—"

Sommers drew close enough to command the jury's attention, but not close enough to draw a charge of intimidation.

"You 'self-assigned' yourself to investigate an unsupported allegation of wrongdoing in a remote part of the state—an area that your newspaper was about to eliminate from its coverage area. You didn't use a local reporter who knew the area and reported to you. You didn't tell your superiors what you were doing. You did all this at an extremely busy time with lots of demands on your attention. Why? Was it that you saw in these documents you'd received in an unmarked envelope the opportunity to earn something you'd always craved, but had never received—a *Pew*-litzer?"

"Absolutely not."

"And so intent were you on bagging this prize that you ignored all evidence that didn't support the conclusion you had determined at the outset, didn't you?"

"Objection, Your Honor!" Miner had been screaming this throughout Sommers' diatribe.

Judge Yates had all three attorneys approach the bench. There were two minutes of muttering among them. I couldn't make out all they said, but the gist was that my team was accusing Sommers of testifying rather than questioning and introducing facts not in evidence. I didn't hear the ruling, but when Sommers resumed, he did not repeat the question.

"One more thing, Mr. Rudberg, where were you on the night of November 4, 2008?"

"Election night?"

"Yes. There was a statewide race for the US Senate, three other important races being decided within the state, several significant ballot initiatives. It was a big night in Oregon. Where was the political editor of the state's largest newspaper on that newsworthy evening?"

"In Chicago."

"With *Obama*," he said, drawing out the name of the president-elect as though it were a curse word. "With all this going on in Oregon, you were in Chicago. With *Obama*."

"Objection, your honor," Miner said. "Where his newspaper assigned Mr. Rudberg the night of the presidential election has no bearing on a story published two weeks before."

"I withdraw the question," Sommers said, his effort to poison those members of the jury who had voted for Senator McCain—or who couldn't stand to see a black man in the White House —complete.

I thought my ordeal was over, but Miner had five questions on redirect. "Mr. Rudberg, what was your motivation in undertaking this investigation?"

"From what someone had given me, it was possible that taxpayers in Franklin County and the State of Oregon were being victimized by a system of payoffs in exchange for inflated government contracts. I wanted to determine if this was true and, if so, tell taxpayers about it."

"In going about your work, were you motivated by any personal animus toward Mr. Allston?"

"No. I didn't even pay attention to the story at first. I didn't know the man and had no opinion about him."

"Why did you report this story instead of assigning someone to it?"

"Because the original material was addressed to me, and in

covering Senator Smith, I was in the area. Once I'd begun, I met with my source. He trusted me, so no one else could take the lead."

"To what degree were you motivated by a quest for a national journalism award?"

"Not at all. I don't even display the AP awards in my office. I don't do this work hoping to receive honors. The pay is good, but otherwise the work is largely thankless."

"In retrospect, is there anything in your story you would change?"

"Not a word. The testimony we've heard over the past few days has only confirmed the accuracy of my reporting."

"I'm sorry, Alan," McAllister said over dinner. "I didn't see that coming. We thought he would go after your reporting. This attack on your motivation—"

"And the racist appeal to the jury—" Miner added.

"We were blindsided. We should have prepared you for something like this."

"I figured it out about the time he asked about the party conventions," I said. "If we'd spent all day rehearsing it, I would have given the same answers."

"There is a positive side to all this. Yates overruled us five times when he should have ruled in our favor, notably on the admissibility of your interview recordings. If the jury goes against us, we're headed right to the court of appeals, and we'll win."

I asked what our chances were. When one of the two was asking questions, the other had been watching the jury.

"It will be close," McAllister said. "Number 7 is on Allston's side, has been since opening arguments. Every time Sommers scored a point today, he got this nasty little grin. Number 11, however, scowled at him when he dragged Obama's name into it and nodded her head when Asa raised his objection."

"Sommers' entire approach today was to play on the Two Oregons," I said. "He wasn't just trying to discredit me. He wanted to remind jurors how much they resent big, bad Portland. Set against the defeat of Eastern Oregon's first US Senator in a half-century by a liberal Portlander, it's a powerful argument."

They didn't disagree. I called Stephanie before turning in, giving her a digest of the day's events.

"But you'll come out on top, won't you?"

I told her I thought so with more assurance than I felt.

"Have you seen the *New York Times* today?"

"No, I haven't read a thing."

"They did a story on one of our factories in the Philippines. It's overblown, but I have to head out there tomorrow morning to fix things. I don't know how long I'll be."

I wished her luck, but once we disconnected, I thought about what she'd told me. An East Coast newspaper had investigated working conditions at an Oregon company's Asian factories. My first reaction was sardonic amusement at Jake Sommers trying to make a big deal out of my reporting a story in Franklin County.

My second was frustration. We should have had that story.

On Friday morning, Jake Sommers began closing arguments for the plaintiff. He came dressed in a suit and tie, which was out of character but made a statement about the importance of what he was about to say.

He thanked the jury and said, "This is a simple case. It concerns an effort by a reporter for a newspaper three hundred miles away to burnish his reputation by destroying that of a dedicated public servant."

He wandered from the jury box to stand behind Brill Allston, who sat with hands folded before him in a cloak of verisimilitude— that and a rumpled suit that looked twenty years old.

"You all know my client." He launched into a detailed rendition of Allston's life and career in Franklin County, working backward from his parentage to the arrival of his great-grandfather three generations before in what was not yet the State of Oregon, then working forward from his birth to the present, through his public schooling to his collegiate years at Oregon State University—"Eastern Oregon wasn't yet a college, let alone the great university it is today"—and his management, with his brother, of the ranch that bore their name. Missing was that they'd inherited the spread from their father, and that much of the land on which they raised cattle was federal property, administered by the Bureau of Land Management. This, the jury was to believe, was a self-made man.

"Y'all know how much money is made in ranching, at least during the good years. Brill Allston could have stayed working the range he so loves, but ten years ago he offered himself for public service. You elected him to the county commission and then as commission chairman. During the past decade he's done much for this county—for you and for me."

Sommers enumerated every road repaved, every mile of pipe laid, every public service offered during Allston's term in office, as though the commissioner alone were responsible. He listed all the boards on which Allston served, all the fraternal and civic organizations to which he belonged, every charitable contribution he'd ever made. Here, his verbal portrait suggested, was one selfless, rock-solid citizen.

"Early this year with the retirement of the senator from his district, Commissioner Allston stepped forward and offered to succeed him." Interesting, I thought, how often running for office is characterized as an egalitarian activity rather than a naked quest for power.

"He was running an honest, positive campaign, depicting a vision for Franklin and our surrounding counties that will create a prosperous future for our vibrant region while preserving the quality and values we cherish. And then came this man."

He stood before the jury, turned to face me, and extended a long arm at the end of which was an accusatory index finger. "Mr. Alan Rudberg, an editor of a newspaper so embedded in the concerns and beliefs of the great urban sprawl to the west of us that, as you heard yesterday, they've decided they no longer need to serve little, insignificant Franklin County."

Sommers turned to face the jury. "Nevertheless, Mr. Rudberg, who had time to follow four major campaigns for national office during a ten-week period and who spent election night in faraway Chicago with Obama and his crowd—Mr. Rudberg found the time to come all the way out here to dig up dirt on this fine public servant."

Sommers nodded in my direction, willing them to remember his cross-examination of the day before. "He allowed a disgruntled county clerk who supported Mr. Allston's opponent to lead him—a mole, if you will. Rudberg took everything this angry man fed him and accepted it as Gospel. And when he printed his allegations, not once did he mention that his source"—Sommers turned the word into a curse—"operating in the dark from a position of anonymity, had contributed to young Nate Pearson's campaign. There's your unbiased reporter at work.

"And what did he find? Hal Meredith paid for a shipment of beef that will be delivered this spring. Rudberg turned that into a bribe. You heard SIL-vee-oh Ber-NARD-oh from way out in Baker City," he said, emphasizing the foreignness of the contractor's name, "describe how he built a pool for Mr. Allston's brother, admitting that Mr. Allston had never asked for one; defendant Rudberg turned that into a bribe. You heard George Smithers, a contractor from up in Pendleton, tell how he brought a campaign contribution to Mr. Allston, a cash contribution that so shocked my client, he never put his hands on it. The defendant turned that into a bribe."

Sommers approached the jury box and spread his arms wide. "You heard five honest, hard-working businessmen who've worked for the county over many years tell about their relationship with my client, the straightforward, businesslike way in which he's conducted their transactions, never asking for as much as a stick of chewing gum.

Did defendant Rudberg report any of this? Did he even visit these men during his four in-and-outs to Central City? No, he was too busy for that. And it didn't fit his narrative. You heard reporter Traci Jacobs describe how the defendant edited her stories to insert things that made my client look bad and remove anything that favorably depicted him. Again, there's your unbiased reporter at work."

He again pointed a long finger at me. "Why did he concoct this story? You heard his attorney trot out all these awards he's won, yet you heard him belittle their significance. He doesn't even display them in his office, he tells us. On closer examination, you heard they're only regional awards, given by local reporters to other local reporters. The defendant has never won a national award. But here was his chance—his opportunity to win a *Pew*-litzer, that most sought-after prize among journalists.

"With these campaigns in high gear, defendant Rudberg left the Obama and McCain campaigns to come to rural Franklin County and win himself an award. Well, we know who deserves an award. These false accusations written by defendant Rudberg and printed by the big-city newspaper that employs him damaged Mr. Allston's reputation. You saw through this vile smear. You reelected him by a wide margin, but my client had to interrupt his campaign to respond, reaching into his own pocket to correct the record. The lies in that article will follow him wherever he goes and preclude his running for higher office to represent Eastern Oregon.

"Unless," Sommers said, "you grant him the relief we seek in this lawsuit. You," he said, planting both hands on the jury box, "can give an award to someone who deserves it. I know you'll do your duty."

After a fifteen-minute break, it was our turn to summarize for the jury, and the job fell to McAllister, who could try to match Sommers' appeal to provincialism with his own rural Oregon roots. He repeated the description of a reporter's role with which he had opened the week before, that it was my job to report what I found and represent ordinary citizens who could not question public officials on their own.

"Mr. Sommers asks why my client would come to Franklin County to investigate potential wrongdoing by a county commissioner. The answer is that it affected every taxpayer in Oregon. The funds that pay for county road repairs come from state grants. So if a county official solicits a bribe to award a contract that is higher than it needs to be, we all pay, whether we live in Franklin County, Multnomah, or Clatsop County on the Oregon Coast. *We all pay.*

"But there's another reason Mr. Rudberg came here to report a story. Mr. Sommers would have you believe Franklin County is too insignificant, too unimportant to merit the attention of a major newspaper. He also maintains that whatever was going on here was of sufficient importance to earn journalism's most prestigious award."

Turning to Sommers, McAllister said, "You can't have it both ways. Which is it? Is Franklin County insignificant, as Mr. Sommers suggests, or is what happens here of consequence to every citizen of this state and to anyone in the nation who cares about good government? I say the latter."

McAllister listed each of the allegations I'd reported in the article and supported each of them. "Hal Meredith first said he'd never paid Mr. Allston $24,500, that the invoice showing the bogus purchase of beef was a forgery. You heard him testify to that 'so help me, God.' When confronted with our handwriting expert, he admitted the invoice and the payment were legitimate, but that the beef just hasn't been delivered. I don't know about you, but when I go shopping for groceries, I bring 'em home with me."

His line got an appreciative chuckle from a few members of the jury, but the rest sat stoically. One looked at his watch, willing this ordeal to end. McAllister noted this and increased his speed. The swimming pool was a fact, he said. Allston had wanted it, he'd gotten it, and only then had Silvio Bernardo received his contract, a full month after submitting the low bid.

The $2,000 cash payment was a fact, only reported as a campaign contribution after my story ran and Allston filed suit. In editing Traci's stories, I had only done my job as an editor. She was upset over losing her job and lashed out, inventing portions of her narrative, which showed why she lacked the temperament and ethical grounding to investigate a story of this magnitude.

The witness who had testified to my conversation with Nate Pearson had heard only part of it, misinterpreted what he did hear, and added something I'd never said. Pearson had appeared and testified that I'd never threatened Allston in his presence and that we hadn't worked together.

The story had not hurt Allston. He'd made previous loans to his campaign and later repaid himself. He hadn't done so in this instance in order to bolster his lawsuit; the money was available in his campaign fund any time he wished to withdraw it. And his letter to voters was something he'd sent every month since launching his campaign.

"Mr. Sommers says this case is simple. It is. There are two questions before us. First, whether Mr. Rudberg's report that Mr. Allston received payoffs for county contracts is true; the evidence shows it is. But even if the story had been inaccurate, the larger question is whether Mr. Rudberg knew it to be false and went ahead, reporting it recklessly and maliciously; that answer is a resounding no."

McAllister assumed the same position as Sommers had, placing both hands on the jury box and leaning toward them. "Franklin County is on trial today. Will you uphold the right of Americans to hear the truth from their journalistic representatives, or will you heed the call of mindless provincialism while rewarding wrongdoing from your public officials?"

He took two steps back and spread his arms to encompass the room. "Our community will always need accurate information and fresh insight on controversial subjects. It is the job of journalists to do that for us. Mr. Rudberg did his job fairly. I ask you to respond with equal fairness by rejecting this groundless lawsuit and its senseless attack on the truth. I know you will."

———

At Noon, Judge Yates issued instructions to the jury who retired to consider their verdict over lunch. We sat in a small office off the courtroom where we'd taken most of our breaks, ordering in sandwiches. There was no reason now not to leave the courthouse and brave the public, but we felt isolated after Sommers' conclusion and preferred the comfort of each other's company.

It was a cold, dreary day, and the three of us shivered as frigid dampness seeped through the walls. McAllister had done a good job, and I told him so. "Parts of those remarks could serve as a text in j-school," I told him.

But Sommers had been scathing and effective, playing to regional prejudice, distrust of perceived elites, and the sense of exploitation shared by those in this rural county.

"The evidence does not support their contention," Miner said. "You did not misrepresent the facts, nor did you act with malice."

However, Oregon civil procedure requires only a nine-member majority to find for either side, and I feared that Sommers' impassioned plea had been enough to persuade that many to vote with prejudice rather than evidence.

Most attorneys believe that the longer the jury is out, the better it is for the defense. However, none of us felt encouraged when a clerk knocked on our door to tell us the jury was about to return. Our bag of sandwiches sitting on the table unopened, we walked into the courtroom in time to see Sommers emerge from Judge Yates' chamber behind the courtroom. What the hell had they been discussing without our counsel present? Miner grimaced, unable to conceal his anger as he scribbled on his notepad.

The jury filed in; no one looked in our direction. Judge Yates asked if they had reached a verdict, and the foreman replied that they had. She handed their verdict to the clerk of court, who passed it to the judge. He opened the paper and allowed himself a slight smile.

"The jury finds for the plaintiff by a vote of 9-3," he said. Although I had suspected this, I sat rooted to my chair, feeling my blood pressure either drop or skyrocket. Allston and Sommers, meanwhile, high-fived each other. Allston smirked.

In the chaotic clash of emotions that ricocheted through my brain like steel balls in a pachinko machine, I did not hear Judge Yates announce that the jury had awarded Allston not only $20,000 in compensatory damages but also an additional $230,000 in punitive damages.

After he dismissed the jury, #7 approached our table. We'd seen him as an Allston supporter from the opening arguments, and Miner stood as though to deflect any confrontation he had in mind. He stuck out a hairy paw that I took reluctantly.

"This is a travesty," he said. "I admire you for what you did. This crowd has had taxpayers in its grip for as long as I can remember. I'm sorry so few of my fellows recognize that."

We later learned that Juror #11, the woman we had found so sympathetic, had led the effort to tack on punitive damages. "I hate newspapers, and I hate reporters," she said in the jury room. "Let's make them pay."

At the moment, I felt cold, devoid of emotion, and isolated. In my mind, they had found me guilty of doing my job. I scarcely heard the reassurance McAllister offered me. "Don't worry, Alan. We'll win this on appeal." I knew that nothing, not even a ruling by the US Supreme Court, would ever make me feel I had won or erase my conviction that I had let Ralph Weaver down.

CHAPTER TEN
JANUARY 18-31, 2009

W e snagged the only three seats remaining on the last flight out of Pendleton. Arriving in Portland a little after seven o'clock, I shook hands with the attorneys and took light rail into town, walking up the hill from the Goose Hollow station to our home. Stephanie had decamped for Manila but left no message.

I had called Bartley Townes from Pendleton. He had already learned of the verdict from Doons Bradbury. I tried to discuss next steps with him, but he put me off. "Don't worry about it," he said. "It's a travesty; we all know it. We're preparing a story for the morning edition, but won't have any other public comment on it. We'll discuss it next week."

"Bart, am I in trouble?"

"No. It was a solid story. The case shouldn't have gone to trial there—not in that town and not before that judge—but there's nothing we can do about it now."

"Except appeal," I said.

"We'll figure all that out next week. Like I said, don't lose sleep over it."

I told him I was exhausted, wrung out, and depressed, and I

asked for a few days off. "Good idea. You have it coming. Take as much time as you need."

I promised to see him Wednesday, and we rang off. I emptied the contents of my suitcase into the washing machine and went upstairs to gather a few items for the weekend. A half-hour later, I headed out Burnside Avenue to US 26, reaching Gearhart ninety minutes later. After dropping my things inside the door of our condo, I headed to dinner at the town's one restaurant. When I returned an hour and a half later, I fell into bed and slept for twelve hours.

The Oregon Coast has always had a cathartic effect on me, enabling me to shut the doors and turn off my mind. We had a burst of warm weather, not unusual for January, and I prowled the beach wearing only a light jacket. I bought groceries from the small market in town and fish from a shop in Seaside, cooking for myself through the weekend, watching English soccer Sunday morning, and making a production of doing nothing at all.

Driving the ten miles north to Astoria Monday morning, I hiked the length of the Riverwalk, from Pier 3 in the heart of town to Tongue Point and back, a twelve-mile round trip. I sat at the bar at the Columbia Cafe and watched the owner-chef, trained in New Orleans, prepare seafood dinners from scratch. He'd acquired a rare Columbia River sturgeon and ladled slices cooked in onion and peppers over fresh fettuccine.

On Tuesday, I watched Barack Obama's inauguration on the small TV I'd swiped from our bedroom at home. Opening my notebook computer, I wrote a column for the following day's paper, laying out the financial challenges that would dog his efforts to enact domestic programs and predicting a rough road through Congress, even with a Democratic majority in both houses. It wasn't prescient; any fool could see it coming.

The two hours I took to write, edit, and file the piece before driving home was the first and only time I thought about work all weekend. Once I turned onto US 26, however, the magic of the Coast disappeared and all my concerns flooded back. For the first time since I'd spoken to him Friday afternoon, something in Bart's response to my questions bothered me. *Don't worry about it. There's nothing we can do about it now. We'll figure it all out later. Take as much time as you want.* It was too casual, not at all typical of his Type A personality, but why I was uneasy, I couldn't say.

No one met my gaze when I entered the newsroom. Eyes remained fixed on screens, phones were held to ears, grunts were returned to my greetings. I was a pariah, a *dalit*.

I dialed Bart Townes' extension. He typically picked up his own phone when I called, but this morning his secretary answered. I asked when I could see him. "He's in a meeting now," she said.

"Well, when he gets back—"

"I don't know when he'll be down," she said. "He's been upstairs every day for the past week."

Upstairs. The fifth floor. For a week. The sixth sense that serves me so well shrieked in my ear. I wasn't imagining things.

The *Examiner* carried my column above the fold, opposite the editorial page. Bart wouldn't have run it if I were on the way out. I called our beleaguered Capitol bureau chief but got no answer. We had halved her bureau on the eve of the legislature's biennial session. I left a message offering to drive to Salem and pitch in for the rest of the week.

I dealt with correspondence, sent notes to two reporters, then walked out into the newsroom, forcing people to speak.

"Tough luck," Dave Madden said. We had joined the *Examiner* in the same year. I'd advanced, while he'd peaked as a local reporter working beats from police to city hall. He had reason to resent my success and to feel *schadenfreude* at my comeuppance, but he hadn't before and didn't now. "It was a BS decision."

"The attorneys assure me there's plenty of reversible error. We'll appeal."

"Great," he said. Then, "Do you have any idea what's going on?"

"No. What do you mean?"

He looked over his shoulder as though someone might overhear him. "It's been weird around here. The execs tiptoe around as though they're afraid of stepping on a landmine. No one picks up his phone. I can't get answers to anything."

"I haven't a clue," I said. "If there's a loop, I'm out of it."

"Honest?"

"Dave, if I knew something and couldn't tell you, I'd say so."

"I know you would." He shook his head while I returned to my office.

I called Asa Miner, but his assistant said he was out. I asked that he call me, then dialed Ben McAllister. I was on hold for ten minutes before he came to the phone. After an exchange of pleasantries, I said, "Have we filed an appeal?"

His pause was almost palpable. "Hasn't Marge spoken with you?"

I explained that I'd taken two days off. "Well, you need to see her. She's handling everything going forward. We're off the case."

"Off the case? Are they blaming you for the verdict?"

"No, that's not it. Alan, I wish I could help, but the *Examiner* is our client. I can't reveal the substance of our conversations. Talk with Marge."

I took the stairway two steps at a time and burst into her office. Her assistant said she was in conference. "In that endless meeting in the conference room? Get her out of it."

The assistant looked shocked, as though no one had ever spoken to her that way. "You heard me. I want to talk to her. Now."

I sat down in the only guest chair in the assistant's office. "I'll wait all day, if that's what it takes."

She stared at me until, convinced I was serious, she left her desk, returning less than a minute later. "Mrs. Cason wants you to wait in her office." She opened the door to admit me but left it ajar, perhaps fearing I would rummage through Marjorie's papers. There was little chance of that. Her desk was clean, all the files secured in the cabinets beneath the shelves of law books.

I waited five minutes, ten, half an hour. The capital bureau chief called my cell phone. "I appreciate your offer to come down," Nadine said. "I need all the help I can get."

Marjorie Cason entered her office, scowling at me. "Are you all right?" Nadine said.

"I'll know in a few minutes." I ended the call.

"What's the meaning of this?" Cason stood behind her chair, her diminutive frame appearing even smaller when framed by the wall of books.

"That's what I'd like to know. Ben McAllister tells me he hasn't filed an appeal and has been removed from the case. He's surprised you haven't told me. So tell me."

She took a deep breath. "You weren't here Monday or I would have sat down with you."

"Ever heard of a telephone?"

"You need to calm down."

"I need to be told what it is I need to know. This trial was bullshit. The judge met with Allston's attorney while the jury was out. Neither McMillan nor Miner were there. By Miner's count, the judge overruled at least five objections he should have sustained. Why haven't we filed an appeal?"

"I prefer that Bart be part of this conversation."

"Then get his ass in here," I said.

She fixed me with a stare that could have drilled through steel, but when she saw I wasn't budging, she left the room, returning a few minutes later with Bartley Townes in tow. "What do you think you're doing?" he said. "We're in the middle of an important planning meeting, and you barge in trying to throw your weight around. You don't have that much weight at the moment, in case you haven't figured that out."

"Cut the crap, Bart. Why isn't Doons Bradbury working on an appeal?"

"The *Examiner* has decided not to appeal, Alan. It's as simple as that."

I gawked at him. There's no other word for it. My mouth hung open; I made no effort to mask my astonishment. "What utter bull—"

"The board made the decision, not us. The quarter-million is well within our insurance limits. It will raise our rates, but—" He shrugged as though the money were of little consequence. "Going to the appeals court only keeps the story alive. Have you seen *Portland Weekly* this morning?"

I hadn't. The *PW* likes to roast us whenever it can. "I can't believe you're doing this to me."

"It's not about you," Marge said.

"It damned well is. This ruling tarnishes my reputation. For the rest of my working days, I will be the reporter whose story produced one of the few adverse media libel judgments in a half century. You're letting me down."

Bart sighed. "I'm sorry, Alan, but they have decided it, and there's no way we can change it. You'll get past this. We all will. Why don't you take some vacation?"

"Why don't you take a flying leap? This is why you were so eager for me to head for the Coast when we spoke on Friday. You wanted me out of the way so you could screw me."

Before leaving for Salem, I picked up a copy of *Portland Weekly*. Far from rubbing it in, Josh Zydell had treated us well. While reporting the facts of the jury's decision, he had made clear we had proven the essential facts in my story. I had no idea where he'd obtained his information—he hadn't been in the courtroom for any part of the trial —but in taking pains to report the full story, Josh and the *PW* were showing solidarity with a fellow journalist. An attack on one was an attack on all. Perhaps Townes was annoyed the *PW* had run any story, no matter how supportive.

I spent the next day and a half working the state capitol. Nadine offered me two important senate committees, but I took the house side, not wanting to run into Brill Allston. Not that I was ashamed; I'd done nothing wrong. I feared my reaction of he fixed that smirk on me.

Salem is close enough that I spent the next two nights at home, commuting to the Capitol each morning. When the last legislative bird left the nest at noon Friday, I wrote up two stories and headed back to Portland.

Ben McAllister had agreed to meet me after work. We ordered glasses of wine at the Heathman Hotel, the Grand Central Station of Portland movers and shakers. The Governor was seated two tables away, so I kept my voice down, but, unlike almost any other bar in the city, the Heathman is quiet enough that two people can carry on a conversation without having to shout.

"The *Examiner* won't appeal. I'm sure you know that. I want to do so on my own."

Ben winced and combed his hair back with his hands. "You can't do that. The cost would be prohibitive. If I were in private practice, I'd take it on *pro bono*, but I work for Doons Bradberry, and our relationship is with the paper."

"What if I—"

"That's the other thing," he said, forestalling my question. "The lawsuit was against the *Examiner*. Despite Sommers continually referring to you as *the defendant*—the correct term is respondent, as you know—it was the paper that published your story; the action was against them. You don't have standing."

But, but, but... I posed several questions, trying to find a pathway through the legal bramble, but Ben was firm. I couldn't do this on my own.

Stephanie returned Saturday morning exhausted. I let her sleep most of the day but woke her up for a dinner of petrale sole in lemon sauce. She poked at it, thanked me for it, but said she wasn't hungry. She went back to sleep at eight but was wandering the house when I arose the following morning, having been up half the night. What had become of her claimed time zone adaptability?

Over breakfast I learned all she was willing to tell me about her trip. "I have to move a contract to another factory," she said. "You people think we don't care about our workers. We do."

"'You people?'" I said. "Who's that?"

"You know what I mean. The press often oppresses."

I let it go unchallenged. She hadn't asked how my week had gone, but I told her.

"I already know."

"You know? How?"

"Mark Fisher sent me an email Sunday. Or was it Monday? I lose track of time."

Mark Fisher again. "Did he also tell you the paper won't appeal?" He couldn't have. He didn't know. I explained the board's decision and how it puzzled me.

"That's shitty," she said. "Disloyal. What will you do?"

I explained why I had no recourse unless I could lobby members of the newspaper's board, something I'd been toying with.

"It's a good thing you signed that agreement."

"Stephanie, this has no effect on our assets—zero. The suit was against the newspaper, and insurance covers the loss."

She sighed as though giving up on a petulant child. "Alan, I'm too tired to discuss it."

And that was the end of our conversation. It turned frosty at our house that week, and I don't just mean the weather.

I stopped by the newsroom Monday morning before heading to Salem. Dave Madden waylaid me before I'd reached my desk. "I guess we'll have answers soon enough," he said.

I was clueless and said as much. "Didn't you get the notice? There's an all-staff meeting at ten." I opened my interoffice mailbox and saw the terse notice, flagged as important. My assistant editor and I went through the week's news budget as we always do Monday morning, but neither of us could focus on what stories were likely to loom large and where we should devote our reduced staff of journalists. Neither of us asked what the other thought the meeting might concern. We had no information, and there was no point in sharing our ignorance.

A few minutes before ten, we walked into the newsroom, already packed with members of all departments—editorial, accounting, commercial, even two supervisors from the print department. Despite the press of bodies, the room was quiet, all of us lost in our thoughts.

Jason Fowler, the publisher, entered a few minutes later accompanied by Gerald Taylor, the chairman of the board. Whatever this was, it was significant. Fowler welcomed us and thanked us for coming as though we had a choice in the matter. I looked at the faces of those around me. No one smiled. I could sense the tension. All of us had seen colleagues leave the week before Christmas, facing uncertain futures as they maneuvered through a shrinking profession in an economy teetering on the brink of depression. Would we soon follow them? Would our salaries be cut? How would we feed our families, put our kids through college, save for retirement? Pay for a condo I shouldn't have bought at a time like this?

"For over a century, the *Oregon Examiner* has been an independent voice for the Northwest, locally owned and managed, reporting to a board of community leaders..."

Oh, Lord. From Fowler's opening words, I knew what was coming. I listened with half a mind while the other half raced. Times have changed. Rising costs. Independent operation no longer practical. Cost of overhead too high. On and on he went, arriving finally at the destination—which I feared was only a way station en route to somewhere else.

They had sold the *Examiner* to a group I'd never heard of, Weyland Media. "This is a good thing for all of you," Fowler said.

"We've been losing money, fighting to maintain a quality product in the face of lower ad revenue and a challenging economy. Although Weyland Media is a new company, they have significant financial resources. Over the past year, they've purchased twelve independent newspapers, a small chain in the Midwest, and seven television stations. They are negotiating with many more media outlets. They will bring economies of scale to the management end of our enterprise so that they can invest more in the editorial and production side."

Those around me relaxed, but I suspected it was bullshit. The *Oregon Examiner* had always been half business, half public servant. We did things that made no economic sense but that served the information needs of our readers. I doubted a new media conglomerate would focus on anything but profit.

No one was safe. None of us would be better off. The *Examiner* would become a different animal.

I left the office before my colleagues could ask questions. Whether I liked it or not, I was part of the management team, and I didn't want to undermine the narrative the publisher had concocted. Neither did I want to lie to those with whom I worked. I was the man who knew too much, and I was grateful to take refuge in Salem.

Somewhere around Wilsonville, the dominos fell. Fowler, Taylor, Cason, Townes—they'd known about this for weeks—for months, now that I recalled that day in November when they summoned me for a rare Saturday meeting that couldn't wait until the following Monday.

Last month's staff cuts had been part of the package demanded by the new owner. *Cut the fat. Lower your expenses. Balance costs with revenue, or the deal's off. You do the dirty work beforehand so we don't have to.*

Every dot and dash my senses had telegraphed were there to see.

I only had to decode them. All the unanswered phone calls Dave Madden had mentioned. The week and a half of fifth-floor meetings where they negotiated the details, the board trying to cut the best deal possible—the best deal for them—making certain their stock held value in the transfer even if our investment of time and talent went down the drain.

Then there was Alan Rudberg and that messy little lawsuit. *End it. Get rid of it. We don't want it hanging over us when we take over.* Which meant no appeal of the judgment, no matter how meritorious our case. *Close it. Get it off the books.* Send Rudberg off to the Coast so he can't see what's going on. Get him out of the way and end the lawsuit so we can close this deal.

It's not about you. Marjorie Cason's words. How right she was. It was not about me or anyone else who worked for the paper. It was about getting the deal done.

CHAPTER ELEVEN
AFTERMATH

What did I do about it? Nothing. I showed up, did my job, and went home each night. I had no choice. Jobs like mine were diminishing, and I had fifteen years before I could consider retirement.

I found things our readers needed to know, investigated them, wrote the stories, edited the work of my reporters, and prepared a twice-weekly column that attempted to put the events we reported into context.

Bradley Townes took early retirement, pocketing a sweet bonus. Frank Sherman, a managing editor from a smaller Weyland Media property, replaced him. He tried to speed up our work, assigning fewer investigative reports and more quick takes. He put less emphasis into print and more into the paper's—they tried to make me stop using that word—the *media's* website.

The *Examiner* moved out of its big building uptown and into a smaller facility near the river. Weyland Media sold the printing presses to a new company in Vancouver. The low hum and odor of ink that had found its way from the press room to the most remote corners of the building disappeared, and with them, the soul of the enterprise.

Sherman installed a huge monitor at the front of the newsroom. It displayed "clicks"—readers on the website opening certain stories—and the time spent with each. These measures replaced quality as the new currency of journalistic achievement.

He pushed for greater productivity—more stories, not as deep. It was like working in a TV newsroom: live shots in front of buildings where fires no longer raged, or on highways where fatal accidents had been cleaned up; few details, but "we'll have more as we learn it."

Three months after purchasing the *Examiner*, Weyland Media reduced the newspaper's format to tabloid size in an attempt to conceal a thirty percent drop in column inches. Home delivery was reduced to four days a week. While we supplied a limited run to newsstands for the remaining three days and offered an electronic edition the full seven days, I considered us no longer a daily newspaper.

On the same day, Weyland Media announced another round of layoffs and ended coverage of arts and culture. Three months later, they laid off another five percent of the editorial staff. Every successive quarter brought another exodus, usually of older, accomplished reporters to make room for youngsters who lacked the experience to do in-depth reporting but were adept at producing quick clickbait stories that became the *Examiner's* electronic bread and butter.

I still did real reporting occasionally. I won two more AP awards, and in 2011 my team won a national award for uncovering a purchasing scam in the city's parking enforcement department. The award was a Pulitzer, which we pronounced correctly.

Meanwhile, I researched another story, one I knew I'd never be able to publish.

Two months after the verdict in what became known as the Allston affair, I drove out to Central City one weekend while Stephanie was out of the country. A stocky, flabby woman who appeared to be in her late seventies greeted me at the door to her home, which was little more than a cottage. This was Bertha Weaver, to whom her son Ralph had been devoted.

Without his salary, she was destitute, living only on social security. She told me she had emphysema and that Medicare covered only part of her costs. She faced selling her home to pay for her treatment but didn't know where she would then live.

I asked if she believed her son had taken his own life. Never, she said. He was a gentle soul who didn't believe in killing—not the smallest animal and certainly not himself. What, then, had happened? She told me that a week after Ralph had lost his job, he had received a phone call from someone representing a local contracting company who said he was looking for an assistant. The caller offered to come around and meet with him. She couldn't remember the name of the caller or company and wasn't sure Ralph had mentioned it in his last phone call with her, the one in which he'd promised to pick her up for church the following day. She was convinced that this person had murdered him.

I put her in touch with an advisor who could help her to rearrange her finances so she could qualify for Medicaid, and I took her story to the state police. She died before they could interview her or she could qualify for the financial help she needed. I had nothing more to substantiate our shared suspicions and had to drop the story, but I still have the file. Someday Weaver may receive justice.

Oregon elects, rather than appoints judges. While meeting with Mrs. Weaver, I looked into Judge Yates' campaign reports. Almost all local attorneys contributed something to his races—that's how things work in Oregon, as in many other states—but none gave more than Jake Sommers, the most prominent criminal defense attorney in the region.

Sommers contributed at least $2,000 to Judge Yates' campaign at every election, but no one had ever opposed him. It's unclear what the judge is doing with the campaign funds. Through three campaigns, his war chest continues to grow, despite the fact no battle is being fought.

Six months after the trial, the IRS charged Senator Allston's brother, Sid, with income tax evasion. Silvio Bernardo's firm had built a swimming pool on his property, but Sid had never reported it as income. Although Brill Allston was a co-owner of the ranch, his brother was the active partner and he alone was charged. He paid a fine and was put on probation. Neither he nor Senator Allston were charged with anything else. Allston has since been reelected to the state senate and is now a committee chair, a position from which he can direct funds to many projects throughout his sprawling district.

Oregon's Secretary of State investigated Hal Meredith for making political contributions under a false name—having his employees contribute to campaigns under their own names and repaying them. That's a felony under state law, but Meredith got off with a fine, and, as Miner had predicted, he was never charged with perjury for lying about the beef invoice.

Meredith's fine, the IRS action against Sid Allston, and the courtroom testimony validated every word I had written about the case, but the *Oregon Examiner*, under its new ownership, declined to seek an appeal. The judgment that I libeled Senator Brill Allston remains on the books and continues to follow me.

A year after Weyland Media purchased the *Oregon Examiner*, Josh Zydell, the investigative reporter for *Portland Weekly*, returned from lunch to find a thick manila envelope on his desk. It bore a printed mailing label with no return address and was postmarked from Astoria, which he must have found curious since the *PW* did not distribute to the Oregon Coast.

Inside were public documents, copies of sales receipts, internal memos, and press clippings concerning a New York City hedge fund and several of its subsidiary companies. Only one subsidiary would have meant anything to him, but that name would have been sufficiently familiar that I picture him dropping the story on which he was working, silencing his phone, and piecing the odds and ends together. From time to time, he must have whistled to himself or emitted an expletive.

He called me two days after receiving the package and asked me a few questions about Weyland Media. I told him I couldn't comment. From the nervous demeanor of my colleagues in the hours after his call, I knew he was also contacting them.

On the following Wednesday, his story appeared under the headline *Oregon Examiner Strip-Mined by Hedge Fund.*

> Brabson Global Capital, a New York based hedge fund, is methodically stripping the assets of the *Oregon Examiner,* the state's largest newspaper, and at least twenty other newspapers across the country.
>
> Local owners sold the *Examiner* last year to Weyland Media, a wholly owned subsidiary of Brabson Capital. Weyland Media moved the newsroom to an office building overlooking Naito Parkway and sold its former headquarters to another Brabson subsidiary, Colquit Holding Company, for $2.6 million.
>
> Colquit soon sold the property to a condominium developer for $5.8 million. Colquit transferred the 100 percent profit to Brabson, which passed it on to its shareholders. None of it remained on the *Examiner*'s books.
>
> In a related transaction, Weyland sold the *Examiner*'s printing presses to St. Helens Press, another Brabson subsidiary. St. Helens

is a non-union printer, whereas the *Examiner* printing staff had been unionized. The *Examiner* contracted with St. Helens to print its newspaper and two related magazines.

As Weyland Media transferred the paper's assets to the hedge fund and contracted for printing at what experts maintain is inflated pricing, Weyland reduced the *Examiner*'s editorial staff by thirty percent, claiming the reductions were necessary to maintain profitability.

Brabson has replicated this pattern of stripping assets and converting them into profits for its investors at newspapers throughout the country.

"This is one hell of a story," Dave Madden said. "I wonder how Josh came up with it."

"He's a fine reporter," I said.

"He must have found a source. I wonder who it is."

I declined to speculate.

I visit Mother at least once a year. In Cheryl's view, it's insufficient, but it's all I can take. Mother has become the doyenne of her table in the facility's dining room and allows no one to join her coterie without her approval. *Watercressnuts* have been banished from the chicken salad.

As Stephanie has become more prominent in Portland, I have become less so; that, at least, is how I feel as the *Oregon Examiner* has become less relevant to people's lives.

She spends more time on the road while I spend weekends alone on the Oregon Coast. When Steph is home, we frequently entertain —or are entertained. Our friends now are mostly her business contacts—those she needs or who need her for some purpose.

They know about the Allston Affair. Most are sufficiently polite not to mention it, but there is always an undercurrent at these gatherings; I know what they are thinking.

With them, as with my professional career, I am guilty until proven innocent.

THE END

ACKNOWLEDGMENTS

This is a work of fiction. Except for the handful of political figures Rudberg references in his stories, all characters are creatures of my imagination and any resemblance to real individuals is unintended.

All the organizations named in this story are fictitious. There is no newspaper operating as the *Oregon Examiner*. Weyland Media is also fictional. That said, everything I wrote about the decline of the *Examiner* and the takeover by Weyland Media and its holding company is occurring in cities throughout the United States. If you enjoyed this book, please subscribe to your local newspaper while there's still time.

Central City and Franklin and Walker Counties are inventions, while Portland, Austin, and other communities and geographic features in this novel are real. (The Mascall Formation is as stunning as I describe it, and I have stood at the overlook watching thunderheads form to the west.)

The incident Rudberg recalls about Vice President Hubert Humphrey responding to a question concerning the grueling nature of a campaign is real. I posed that question to Humphrey during his unsuccessful presidential campaign in 1968. His response was characterized in a front-page story by the now defunct *Washington Star* as a "love song to America."

This novel is a prequel to my earlier book, *Sins of Omission*. In that novel, the libel judgment forms an important part of Rudberg's background, but even though I had the details in mind, I did not detail the case.

Those who have read both novels will recognize an important difference between them. While *Sins of Omission* was written from the omniscience of third person point of view, I wrote *Breaking News* in Rudberg's voice. From the opening paragraph, I felt that the first-person point of view would give the reader greater insight into his thoughts and personality.

If you enjoyed this story, please leave a review on your favorite site. Reviews are the principal way in which independent writers are discovered by new readers.

I am indebted to my colleagues at Pittsburgh South Writer's Group, who reviewed and commented on the scenes concerning the relationship between Rudberg and his mother and sister.

I thank dozens of colleagues in journalism and public media with whom I have discussed the decline of the daily newspaper during the past decade.

I am particularly grateful to my editor, Kylee Hartwell, CEO of Noteworthy Revisions, whose valuable suggestions found their way into this novel and whose editing skills eliminated the many gremlins who invaded the copy while my back was turned. Kylee previously served as my editor on a major non-fiction project and tackled this novel with equal dedication and professionalism. I recommend her to anyone looking for a talented editor.

The cover design was by Laura Boyle of Laura Boyle Design in Toronto, as well as for all my other books to date. She does terrific work, as you can see.

Finally, to my wife Julie, daughters Kristen and Lisa, and grand-children Caeden and Emma, I offer thanks for your patience and all my love.

ABOUT THE AUTHOR

James H. (Jim) Lewis is a former journalist, public media executive, and consultant who is now a story-teller for nonprofit organizations. This is his third novel. He has lived and worked in Washington, DC, Florida, Texas, Massachusetts, Oregon, and Sweden.

He has written for the *Washington Post, Fundraising Management,* and *Current.* His news reports have aired on public television, the ABC Evening News, and on the Eurovision News Exchange. Jim and his wife, Julie, currently reside in Pittsburgh.

Follow Jim on https://lewisthescrivener.com.

ALSO BY JAMES H LEWIS

Sins of Omission

Novak's Mission